Camille Oster – Author
Instagram: camilleoster_author
Email: Camille.osternz@gmail.com

The Nuisance WIFE

By Camille Oster

Chapter 1:

THE FLOOR SHIFTED SLIGHTLY and the lantern swung above where Caius sat at his desk, signing letters as Lord Warwick for the first time since assuming his late uncle's title. It sat badly with him, but his uncle's death had been inevitable. An aimless ding of the bell up on deck drew his attention to the roughness of the seas.

This cabin had been his home for longer than he cared to remember, but they were coming into port shortly, after having to traverse the rougher seas of the Atlantic.

His trunk shifted slightly along the floor. The seas were rough indeed. It would certainly be bad luck to succumb in a shipwreck so very close to home. Not that he would. Danger for him was an instinct he knew well and he simply didn't feel it now. It was just rough seas.

Six long years since he'd set foot on his own soil, having spent his time as a major, protecting the Queen's interest in the South China Seas. Mostly in Hong Kong and in China. If it wasn't for the duties to the title, he probably wouldn't be returning at all. Life in the orient had suited him perfectly.

"We're off the coast of France," someone said to a companion outside his cabin, which meant they were getting close. But he also knew that the very end of a voyage was the most trying, because one started to think about what to do when off the ship, and suddenly the small spaces of the ship felt confining.

Dropping his pen down on the desk, he rose and paced. Before him lay all the things he'd simply walked away from six years previously. His siblings. His father.

His wife.

With a deep sigh, he paced, feeling he needed more than the small area of his cabin, so he stepped out and made his way up on deck. Strong winds buffeted him as he stepped out into the cool air. They were definitely further north. The warm airs of Africa left behind. Steadily moving toward the cold, rainy isles of Britain.

There had been things he'd missed. Foods and fruit. A good scone with strawberry jam, and the sheer choice of tipples. The selection had been more limited in the orient, and rarely did they have the single malt reserve bins from the smaller distilleries. Not to mention the cognacs and bourbons from France.

But then there were the things he hadn't missed. Particularly the scandal and betrayal, the falsities and pretense and everything that had to do with his wife. Eliza. How fooled he'd been.

Well, it was time to address the issue. Swiftly and succinctly was how he would prefer to do it. How she would prefer to do it remained to be seen. It didn't matter all that much as money and title tended to take precedence in these things.

Over to the right, he could see a few lights in the distance along the French coastline. They really were getting close to home. A day or two and he would be in Southampton, and back on English soil.

*

No one met him at the port, which wasn't surprising as he'd sent no details of his arrival. Likely his brother and father would assume his imminent arrival due to the passing of Uncle Theodore.

"See to some transportation, will you," he said to Mr. Jones before stepping onto the gangplank leading down to the dock. Already, the cargo holds had been thrown open and sacks were being lifted out. They didn't linger, did they? The moment the ship pulled in, the unloading started. Port fees were expensive, he understood, so ships had incentive to be quick.

A jumble of carts stood waiting, and a few carriages standing by to pick up arrivals. People were everywhere, waiting, moving, heaving. Dodging through the frantic activity, and guarding himself against the manure littering the ground, he made his way to the pub he'd seen from the ship.

It felt strange walking on firm land. His body and mind were so used to the relentless shifting under his feet that he now felt strange. Only for a short while as there was a long carriage ride ahead of him. Right now, though, he wanted a drink, for all the things he'd rather not do.

It wasn't as if he feared doing them, it was the betrayal and disgust he didn't want to deal with—had seen no need to deal with it, because none of it had been his doing. But it was time.

The tavern smelled as he walked in, filled with rough furniture and rough men. They knew on sight he wasn't one of them, but they also knew to leave him be. He knew these men, had led men just like them into battle, had worked with them, and occasionally bled with them.

They weren't all good men, but when honor shone through them, it was as bright as he'd ever seen.

Even so, he would never be a part of them, and that went both ways. Grudging respect worked well from everyone.

"A whiskey," he said to the dirty and stained barman. The bar was old and scarred from use. Had been painted blue at some point in its history.

"Which kind?" he said without a smile.

As opposed to what people believed, port taverns, for being rough and uncouth places, usually had an excellent selection of tipple, designed to alleviate newly paid sailors of as much coin as possible.

"The *Craggy Tor special reserve*," he said and barman grabbed a small glass and then the dusty bottle from the top shelf. Caius liked it when the bottles were dusty. It often signified something special.

The honey-brown liquid shone in the poor light. Lovely color. It had been long years since he'd tasted one of these.

Picking the glass up, he brought it to his lips.

"Got a carriage for taking us to London. Or do you wish to head to Denham?" Mr. Jones said, arriving at his side. Jones had an even more quieting effect on the tavern than he had. His visage had that effect with his missing eye and savaged cheekbone, and the absent left arm. People, even the rough ones, didn't dare wonder what hellhole Jones had crawled out of. And it had been a hellhole.

With disappointment, he placed the glass down. It wasn't such a height of joy experiencing this tipple when there was a man waiting impatiently for direction. Despite his missing pieces, Mr. Jones was a good manservant, albeit impatient. Soldiers had their limitations.

"I think London first," Caius said quietly and Mr. Jones walked away.

Returning his attention to the glass he sighed as he brought it to his lips again.

"And where'd you come from then?" a man said, older and of a rough disposition. Pox marks scarred his face. Clearly dumb enough to think that he could have found his next mark.

"From hell," Caius said gravely.

There was a moment of tenseness. He would struggle if the whole tavern decided they wished to claim his purse, which could happen if he had to deal with the pox marked man in a decisive manner.

"Davie, leave him alone," a man called from the crowd. There was a tense atmosphere for a moment, but it stretched too long, long enough so everyone knew that no one was making a move.

The older man slinked away, grumbling as if he'd somehow been prevented from gaining his loot.

Finally he poured the liquid into his mouth and savored the smooth burn. Oh, it was nice. It had been aged perfectly. Flavor filled his senses—taste, burn, scent. Sheer beauty. It reminded him of sunshine, summer days and happiness.

Slowly he opened his eyes and was back in the grubby tavern. "I'll take the bottle," he said and placed down enough coin to cover it and then some.

Taking the bottle, he walked out of the tavern, but it would be a stretch to say into fresh air. The port had a cacophony of unpleasant smells, not helped by livestock from Brittany being unloaded right in front of him.

Searching, he found Mr. Jones, who stood by a carriage. It was well sprung. A good choice for the long ride north.

Damn, he should have bought a glass too, but he hadn't thought of it and unceremoniously drank from the bottle. While, he appreciated alcohol probably more than most, he wasn't beholden to it as some were. It had a time and a place, but this long drive north signified a good time for a bit of indulgence. It was a small pleasure, but there were times, when battle was heavy and it seemed the sun would never come out again, when small pleasures were all one had.

Men had different vices. His was a good whiskey. He might need a few in the weeks ahead.

Chapter 2:

BUCKET IN HAND, ELIZA stood and watched the roof, waiting to see if any of the leaks remained. Workmen had been on the roof all week after she'd pestered her landlord for months on end. Finally the roof had been fixed and her books were safe, but she wasn't going to trust it until she saw it with her own eyes.

"I think it's holding," Teresa said, eyeing the ceiling furtively.

"It seems that way. Well, that is a load off my mind. It would be nice to think we didn't have to run around dealing with leaks all the time. Perhaps we can get on with the Somerset order."

"*The Widows and Orphans Charitable Trust* hasn't given their final approval yet."

With a sigh, Eliza put her bucket down. "What is taking them so long?"

"I gather they only meet once a month and at times they don't get to everyone on the agenda," Teresa said. "I suppose they're not ready to make the purchase yet."

One would think that charities were easy to deal with, particularly when providing school supplies for charitable schools, but some of the people she'd met in these charities were some of the hardest people she'd ever met. Many were entirely well-meaning, but there were a few people for whom Eliza didn't entirely understand why they were there.

Biting her lip, she wondered if she could get the assistance of another charity to provide the materials to the children, but it would be a hard endeavor trying to justify providing charity to children who were firmly in the domain of another particular charity. Charities were surprisingly competitive.

"I suppose we will simply have to wait."

"But in the meantime, I am wondering about the slate that just arrived," Teresa continued. "I'm worried it might be too thick. If a child were to drop it, it could do some damage to unprotected toes."

A fact that Eliza hated was that a number of the children who attended the most meager schools had no shoes. The schools that ran on fees rather than charitable trusts with wealthy patrons. For a long time, she'd wondered if there was some way she could manufacture shoes for these children, but she hadn't managed to find the right materials and production process to make it feasible.

"Then we will have to sell that slate to one of the charity schools," Eliza said. "We will have to look for another source for the slate."

Making her way back to her small office, she went over the accounts and found the purchase of the slate, and calculated what she had to sell it for. The margin they were earning was thin to start with, so she couldn't discount it anymore. This business had its expenses and it had to support the people who made it run. Profit wasn't the purpose, but it had to keep itself alive.

At times, it felt like an endless string of problems, but she loved the small business she'd built. It had given her purpose. Granted, she enjoyed creating the learning books they designed, but it had become a small part of the business. So many things were required to keep it going.

A knock sounded on the door and she looked up to see Tom, their errands boy. "There's a letter for you."

"Really?" The post had already come for the day, so this must be hand-delivered.

Accepting it with an absent smile, she turned it over. *Aberford Law Associates,* it said, and unease crept up her spine. Solicitor involvement never meant anything good. What in the world could this be in regards to? As far as she knew, none of the current dealings involved any disputes that would result in solicitor communication.

Grabbing her penknife, she sliced the fine parchment open and extracted the letter. The paper was so thick, she actually had to hold it open. The language was impossible to understand, but she definitely saw the *1857 Marriage Causes Act* mentioned several times. And also Lord Warwick.

This wasn't about her work. This was about her husband's family. But why would Lord Warwick be mentioned? And then it occurred to her that it was her husband it was referring to. He must have inherited the title.

Again she tried to read it. Dissolution of the marriage, it said. There was also a time and date where her presence was required.

Bringing her hand to her mouth, she dropped the parchment on the table. Her husband was initiating divorce proceedings. In a way, it wasn't a surprise, but it had been so long, she had in many ways forgotten about it—about him. It was a portion of her life she had wished quite firmly to forget.

And now it was here. There would be renewed scandal and trouble, that ill-fated marriage still causing upheaval.

A worse thought occurred to her. Technically, the business she'd built belonged to him. Anything she had belonged to him, including her, and with a divorce, he could take absolutely everything. Not that he would be interested in a small business producing educational material for charity schools, but she could very well imagine him doing so out of spite.

All she had built could be taken away from her. Not to mention that a divorce would make many of the charities she dealt with highly suspicious of associating with her, claiming her character was untenable, even as she was no different a person than the one she'd been a mere hour ago.

Most likely this also meant that Caius was back in England. For a while, she'd believed that she would simply never see him again. He had seemed intent on forgetting their marriage had ever happened, but that was not the case.

Now he had a title and likely his uncle's estate that went with it. He would need an heir and he clearly didn't feel she was suitable as a mother for that heir.

It was an insult, but truthfully, it didn't hurt overly much. So many tears she'd shed for that marriage—she simply didn't have any left. Years had stretched and she'd put the debacle behind her.

"What's the matter?" Teresa asked as she walked into the office. "You look like you've seen a ghost."

"In a way I have," Eliza admitted with a wry smile.

Oh, how was she going to tell Teresa about the risk they now faced? They could lose the company entirely, because again, it technically belonged to her husband.

They might simply have to start a new company after the divorce if Caius wasn't amenable. They had the knowledge and the contacts, although they might lose all their inventory. It would be very difficult to start again, but they might not have any choice. And if her reputation as a divorced woman would be too destructive, perhaps Teresa would have to be the principal. Eliza might have to withdraw entirely.

This was all less than ideal, but both her and Teresa had dealt with setbacks before. The world was a cruel place and the only way in it was to make a place for oneself. Teresa had been filthy and starving with two children tucked under her dirty shawl when they'd met. Something about her defiance had made Eliza stop. And given the chance, Teresa had worked harder than anyone else Eliza knew, because she'd taken the opportunity and made as much of it as she could. So here they were, friends and colleagues.

And now they could lose everything again.

"It will all be fine," Eliza said with more confidence than she felt.

"What will be?"

"My husband has returned."

Teresa's eyebrow rose. "And what does he have to say for himself after all this time?" It could be said that

Teresa's trust in men had been eroded by her experiences. Although she was beautiful, she paid no attention to the men who tried to catch her eye. Eliza understood.

"A petition for divorce," Eliza said and picked up the letter.

The room was silent for a moment. "I'm sorry," Teresa finally said.

"It was perhaps bound to happen." Eliza had hoped this day wouldn't come, but she wasn't entirely surprised it had. "But I think we must make some preparations in case things turn difficult."

Teresa sighed and leaned her hand on the desk, looking out of the stretch of paned windows. "Do you think he'll be difficult? You built this entirely on your own."

"Honestly, I don't know. He was very angry the last time I saw him. I have no idea how he feels now, but it seems he is in need of a divorce. Perhaps he has someone he wishes to marry."

"And he is willing to rip you to pieces to do so."

"So it would appear." The divorce would be scandalous. Every part of it would be reported and salaciously gossiped about. Any standing she held in society, which hadn't been all that good as her husband had deserted her, would be decimated as a divorcée. No doubt the cause for the divorce would be adultery. One accusation that had destroyed her marriage, and now reputation in the broader world. "It is what it is," she said and put the letter down again.

Chapter 3:

THE GREENERY STILL HAD the lushness of late summer, but the clement weather was gone. It rained, a symphony of waterdrops on leaves around. Caius listened to the patter as he traveled along the road leading west. Along with the jingle of the harness and the squeaks of the carriage.

It was too stuffy to keep the windows closed in the carriage, so they were both open, wetness occasionally splattering from the top of the door.

A headache sat at the back of his eyes. A hangover. Friends he hadn't seen in many years insisted on celebrating his return, and one couldn't help but be amenable in such circumstances.

Returning to London wasn't something he wished to celebrate. He'd been there to see his solicitor and start the proceedings against Eliza. Exactly where she was, he wasn't sure, but she had a mailing address in Lambeth, which wasn't exactly a genteel neighborhood. This made him wonder what she was doing with the money he'd sent her every month. Perhaps she was drinking it away in unsavory establishments in Lambeth.

With his name, she had some standing in society, but clearly one she'd lost as she now resided south of the Thames. Perhaps someone like her couldn't help but to seek lower circumstances in life. From what he had seen, she'd achieved it so far.

Putting to side the specter of his wife, he tried to regain the serenity he felt observing nature's symphony outside the window. The scenery was starting to look more and more familiar, which meant he was approaching his childhood home.

Seeing it now, it struck him that he'd missed it—missed the greenery and the sedate country lifestyle. Not that he'd seen it so much before, being distracted by the entertainment in London and then his marriage to Eliza Ellerson—a gentle beauty that had stolen his breath away. It hadn't strictly been a beneficial marriage as her being the daughter of a clergyman, she'd brought little to it. Her brother had inherited the small family house in Kent, with its small lands that did little more than feed his family.

Interestingly, Eliza hadn't returned to her brother after the separation, which showed more clearly that she was an incorrigible figure who sought the diversions of London, and whatever men she associated with.

All in all, it had been a disaster of a marriage, and the worst was that his brother had warned him against her, but he hadn't listened. In fact, he'd fancied himself in love with his pretty wife. How wrong he had been.

Before long, the carriage passed through the nearby village and continued on to Denham Hall. In some ways, he was pleased to see it again, but there were so many competing emotions—some of which had chased him around the length of the world. And things were to get worse, because before long, everyone in England would know exactly how disastrous his marriage had been.

The letter initiating the divorce had been sent, the charges about to be filed. The process, which he fully expected to be grueling and horrific, had now begun.

Then the house appeared as it always did as, as if nestled in a glade, framed by trees and parkland. It was still one of the most handsome houses in the country, and he felt pride as he saw it. But this was his brother's estate and it had always been meant to be. Bickerley House was pretty in its own way, but it was not a house on the magnitude of Denham Hall.

Familiar trees lined the road up to the house, and on approaching he saw that little had changed in the years he'd been gone. Except the ornate, glass-lined building, which he assumed was some kind of orangery.

"Master Caius," Mr. Thomas said as he walked outside. The man, who had been with the family as long as Caius had lived, was older, his hair lightening with age. "We were not expecting you."

"Good to see you too, Mr. Thomas." The man expressed himself with the elevation of his eyebrows and little else, and there had been times when Caius had found himself doing the same thing. If there was ever a picture of stoicism, it was Mr. Thomas. "I take it my brother is home."

"He is," Mr. Thomas confirmed. "Are you staying with us for the evening? If so I will bring in your effects."

"Mr. Jones can assist." Having only one good arm, Mr. Jones sometimes struggled with trunks, but the man always found a way of getting things done. "I assume you can find a place for him?"

"Of course."

"My word," a familiar voice said and Octavia appeared in the doorway, looking exactly the same. "Is that you, Caius? We wondered if we might see you before long, or if you would insist on being negligent with us."

Coming over, Octavia embraced him, smelling exactly as he remembered his sister smelling. Gardenias. It was her favorite scent. "I felt I had to come. You look lovely."

"Julius," she called, but there was no response as they listened. "Heaven knows where he's hidden himself away. Come, we must find him."

"Found," Julius said, appearing on the landing above, looking dapper. His brother always ensured he looked smart. "Well, well. You're back. We were wondering when you'd make an appearance."

"I just told him that," Octavia said.

"Father will be pleased," Julius continued. "Come, you must tell us what you have been doing with yourself all this time. Soldiering, I expect."

Julius's dismissiveness of Caius' career as a soldier was something they had dealt with for years, but Caius knew that jealousy lay at the root of it. As the eldest son, a commission had never been a possibility for him, but his brother had envied his career, the advancement and the respect given to the uniforms Caius often wore. Even now, Caius at times wondered if Julius wouldn't mind terribly if their places were switched. Not that anyone would be ungrateful in being the heir to Denham Hall, with its title and substantial prospects. While a life of comfort and respect, it wasn't one of adventure.

Nothing had changed inside the house, which was comforting, in a way. The furniture was the same and in the exact place he had always known it to be. They walked into the salon and Octavia gracefully draped herself over the chaise lounge. "So I suppose you've had to give up your commission now that you're Lord Warwick."

It was true, but it was the ideal time for it. He wasn't sure how many more battles he could face. The faces around him seemed to be getting younger and every year, more of them seemed to perish. There was a natural stage when one should give it up, and if he hadn't reached it, he would soon. Or else one would become too congruent to function in society, stuck soldiering because one couldn't do anything else.

He was only thirty. Although he felt much older.

"So what are you going to do about *her*?" Julius asked.

"Now that I am back, I will have to deal with her."

"Now that you are Lord Warwick, you cannot simply leave her as your wife and live apart," Octavia said, "to forever live like a bachelor. That might suit some, but you need a proper wife."

Initially when they'd married, Octavia had been the only one who supported the match, had adored the romance of a love match. But it had all turned so wrong. Like him, Octavia had also been fooled. While Julius and his father made out as if they'd expected it all along. Her faithlessness.

At the time, it had taken him completely by surprise, a thunderbolt out of the blue, but the truth had spilled from the very man who'd seduced her. There was no doubt whatsoever. She'd paid heed to his attention, and that heed had turned to passion.

It had pierced his heart, which he feared had died from the wound. It had certainly killed the illusion that had been their marriage. The creature she was had been revealed, and sheer unpleasantness ensued.

As mortifying as it had all been, he had been a man of honor and had supported her throughout, instructing his man of business to diligently send her a sum of money each month. A sum that would not support a life of luxury, but enough for modest rooms and a modest lifestyle.

Clearly she had wished for a more lavish lifestyle as she scrimped on what she paid for her rooms. Who knew what kind of society she dwelled in, but she seemed to have given up all pretense of respectability.

Perhaps that would make the divorce easier, and him more of a laughingstock for choosing such a creature for his wife. He wasn't the first man to be fooled by a pretty face, and like all who were, he was made to suffer for it.

Chapter 4:

"WHERE'S MUMMY?" Rosie asked as Eliza picked a bit of lint off the girl's shoulder.

"She's still at the printery, so I thought I'd pick you up. How was your day?"

"I can walk on my own, you know."

"Your mother would have a fit and perish out of worry."

"I'm not a little child."

"You are still very much a child and these streets are dangerous for an eight-year-old."

Together, they walked out of the school gate and onto the busy streets of Lambeth. Horses and carriages pushed into the crowd, along with carts and sellers of everything imaginable. In some ways, Eliza loved the liveliness of the streets, but at times she missed the more sedate pace of country life. Although she wondered if the pace would be too slow for her now, sitting all day with very little to do. She wasn't quite sure how she'd managed to spend her days as a young woman, or even as a married woman. There had been a lot of tea and chatter with various people.

"Do you want an apple?" Eliza asked and Rosie nodded. The child would probably rather go to the confectioners, but Teresa would not forgive her. Then Eliza would likely get yelled at, like a naughty schoolgirl.

They stopped at a cart and bought two apples, the earliest of the autumn crop was coming in. Fresh apples. Was there anything better, Eliza thought as she bit into hers. They were at times cheap and abundant, and she used them a great deal in the educational material she created, because all children knew what they were.

Without trying to, her mind slipped into her work, thinking of the arithmetic project she'd been mulling over, an intermediate book. They had made a great deal of material for young children to learn letters and numbers, but not as much for older children, and they were now starting to.

"And what would you like to do on Sunday?" Eliza asked, pulling herself out of her train of thought.

"The zoo," Rosie said.

"You want to go to the zoo? Again?" For all her professions that she wasn't a child, she still very much liked the things she'd liked when she was smaller.

"And what do you wish to see this time?"

"The tigers."

"Ah." There was a spirit of adventure with Rosie. She liked feeling scared. Her mother had that same defiance. It kept them in good stead for some things, but not always by means of showing caution. However, it made them work together well, because Eliza was more cautious and Teresa saw the potential. Together, it made them cautiously optimistic.

Then it occurred to her that perhaps they needed to save their pennies in the next while, because all they had could be taken away in this divorce. If not by Lord Warwick, then by the scandal of the divorce itself.

Perhaps in the next little while, and maybe permanently, they should promote Teresa more as the face of the company. But technically, Teresa didn't own the company, Eliza did. Keeping the structure of the company simple had been necessary so as to not involve Caius in this venture. Anything complex and his signature would have been required, and he was simply not around to do that—not that she'd wanted to go beg him for a signature. So a very simple structure had suited her, but that simple structure was now at risk with this divorce.

Truthfully, she hadn't dedicated the time to study the ins and outs of female ownership laws to discover what was possible, if there was some kind of way she could set up a trust without her husband's signature. Perhaps she should have anticipated this day would come.

Then again, she had no idea what Caius' intentions were. Largely, she was utterly at the mercy of how he wished to provide for her. He had provided her with a stipend as they had separated, but a divorce might see him cut ties with her altogether.

He'd certainly been angry the last time she'd seen him. It had been a horrible day. Tense and cuttingly sharp. It hadn't been entirely unexpected as she'd been shunned completely for a few days before, having to retreat to her own room in Denham Hall, then being asked to vacate the property.

It still gave her chills to think about it, the coldness she'd received from him and his family, then being put in a carriage with her trunk, bound for London.

With a sigh, she dismissed the heavy feelings that came with thinking back on those days. It was much more pleasant to think of the things she'd done since, and the fantastic apples they were partaking in. "I wonder what Mrs. Fisher will cook for supper this evening."

"Not more tripe, I hope."

"She hardly ever cooks tripe. The French adore tripe, you know."

"Well, they can keep it."

It didn't take long to get home. In fact, they'd chosen the house because of its proximity. It was a decent house, nothing extraordinary, and the landlord had sought someone to take care of it while he lived overseas.

"Afternoon, Mrs. Fisher," Eliza called when they walked in the door and hung up their coats, entering the relative quiet and stillness of the house compared to the streets outside.

Rosie ran upstairs, while Eliza walked into the parlor and sat down. It was warm enough that a fire wasn't needed, but that would change soon. The nights were cooling down and the mornings were brisk. A good time of year, because the Thames didn't smell so awfully. Summer was when she missed her former country lifestyle the most.

As soon as she sat down, her mind returned to the arithmetic project. Perhaps she shouldn't think so much of work, but it was a darn sight better than thinking about the divorce.

The door opened and the house was noisy, which meant Teresa had to be home with Philip. For some reason, the moment there were two children in the house, it ceased to be quiet.

"Go upstairs and get cleaned up for supper," Teresa said and Eliza saw him pass by the parlor door in a flash. Then Teresa appeared.

"What are you going to do?" she asked.

"About the arithmetic book?"

"No, you goose. Him."

"Well, there's not much I can do. I suppose I will have to get a barrister to argue my case." The moment she said it, she recognized that it would utterly deplete any money she had. Barristers weren't cheap.

Naturally, the charge against her would be adultery. No doubt they would drag out William Castle Garrick to repeat his slanderous accusations. In the light of it, it would be impossible to prove otherwise.

And prove otherwise for what reason, so the divorce was not to be granted? Then they would have to remain married. That was far from ideal as well, but would prevent the scandal that was to come. But to stay married to a man who clearly didn't want her. That was... very uneasy.

"I don't know," she finally said after a while.

"Couldn't you simply not tell him about the business?" Teresa suggested. "If we deplete the inventory, which are our only assets, there is little real value in the business. And if you never bring it up, then maybe he'll never even notice it's there. Ahead of this, we could stage a little fire-sale."

"I might need to just to pay for the barrister."

"The main focus should be after the divorce. That is what's important."

Teresa was always so practical and that's what Eliza adored about her. She never looked back, only to the future. In fact, to the degree that Eliza knew quite little about her past, because she rarely wanted to talk about it. But a standing aversion to men had resulted from it.

"I think after the divorce, we should set up a partnership. You might have to take a more visual role, because my name will be in the mud."

"That will pass, you know. Scandal only hold people's interest for so long."

"True, but a tarnished character is forever." And she certainly knew that was true. It didn't matter if the accusation was true or not, it had bit deeply and affected everything in her life. Her ruined reputation had been a force unto itself, unable to be fought or reasoned with. It had its way with her, but she'd built a life for herself—one that was under threat now.

There had to be some way of protecting what she'd built. And if they depleted the stocks to practically nothing, all they had were contacts, contracts and expenses. Even the profits were not remarkable, because everything she'd earned had gone back into expanding the business.

Obviously things didn't work that way. Businesses were judged on their potential, not the state of their assets. But maybe there were things she could do. How she wished she had someone she could speak to about this. An experienced barrister, but was it even possible to find one who had sympathy for her, a notorious adulteress.

Chapter 5:

THE GARDENS AT DENHAM were past their prime, but still lush as the summer was coming to an end. Caius walked them with Octavia. Unfortunately some said the same thing about his sister, who at twenty-six was considered past her prime and skirting spinsterhood. But she had discerning tastes when it came to whom she spent the rest of her life with, and he wondered if his disastrous marriage had put her off the institution entirely.

Having been away, however, he had no idea what her social engagements had been like. Perhaps she'd turned down beau after beau. Her dowry would attract many. Then again, he didn't know quite a lot about her dealings.

"You haven't become engaged lately?" he asked. Such news could have missed him entirely.

"No," she said and they kept wandering in silence.

It could be a fraught subject to bring up as his sister could become irate when pushed about things she didn't wish to speak about. "There isn't anyone…?" he started.

The blush on her cheeks suggested there might be, which was interesting. Still, it would not do to push his sister further unless she wished to speak.

"What about yourself? Have you had any alliances over in the orient?"

"No time for such things." Besides, all the women that came to the orient tended to be married, and pursuing married women wasn't a game he dabbled in. And for an unattached woman, he presented a messy prospect in that he was still married himself.

With his divorce, that would change, although there would be some women who would shy away from a divorced man. Not to the degree that they would shy away from a divorced woman, and rightly they should in this case.

More topics that seemed fraught to discuss. "You have not heard any news of..." It even felt awkward saying her name. For so long, he had wiped her from his thoughts, but returning here, she was returning to his mind as well. The last time he'd seen her had been here at Denham. "Eliza?"

"Oh, no. I haven't heard a peep actually. She either travels in no society or one entirely different from ours."

"That is what I fear," he found himself saying. He feared something entirely unsavory and it would all come out in the divorce, the bones of this dead marriage being picked over by all of society. And they would all see exactly how poorly he'd chosen his wife. Although fear might not be the right word. Fear was what you felt when you rode into battle, a silent kind of scream inside your head as time slowed down and you truly feared for your life. In comparison, a divorce was nothing to fear. "I worry that it will perhaps be detrimental to your prospects."

"Oh, don't worry about me. I have no interest in a man who wilts."

"No, I suppose one wouldn't want one of those."

"So you haven't heard anything about her?" Octavia asked.

"Other than her address, I know little about her circumstances. Lambeth."

The grimace on Octavia's face showed she agreed it wasn't an address for a respectable woman. "But I will see her, I understand. There is to be a coming together of the parties."

"That should be uncomfortable," Octavia said. "I wonder if she will plead with you. How embarrassing."

Try as he might, he couldn't really see that. Eliza had never pleaded, not even when the accusation had been laid down. Honestly, he didn't remember that much about it. He'd been too distracted by his own distress, but he did recall that she denied it. But of course she would, even as the evidence was glaring and insurmountable. Still, she had denied it and that had hurt the most, the consistent lying.

Perhaps that was what had broken it so completely. If she'd perhaps admitted it, owned her wrongdoings, they could have found some way, but she kept to her lies. Even now he was growing angry, after all this time.

No, he would not enjoy seeing her again. This time was likely to prove trying. Maybe even for all of the family, but no one argued that this was necessary. There was now a title and an estate to support, and for that he needed to be rid of this faithless wife.

Father had arisen by the time they returned to the house, and they awkwardly embraced. Affection was awkward between them, always had been.

Chapter 6:

IT WAS INORDINATELY time-consuming trying to find a barrister to represent her. Eliza had had to go around quite a few of them. Not all had experience with divorce proceedings, and others didn't have the capacity to take her on. She did note quite a distinct chill in how they treated her, and it suggested that her reduced status was something that would stay with her throughout the divorce and beyond. But this had to be faced, there was nothing for it. This marriage was over, so it should be ended.

In the end, she found Mr. Oakwood, who'd agreed to represent her throughout the process. She had been so relieved that she'd finally found someone that she didn't inquire about the cost. She doubted there was much distinction between them—they would all be expensive. Their plan of selling down a good portion of the inventory would free some money for her. If it cost more than her means, she would probably have to go into debt.

The day of the initial meeting referred to in the letter she'd received was fast approaching and she felt nervous. Everything about this whole thing made her feel nervous, mostly because it was entirely out of her control. She hadn't initiated it and had little power over it, it was just something that was happening to her, whether she liked it or not.

This period she would simply have to endure. What was left of her life afterwards she would have to stitch back together, and hopefully continue with the business that had absorbed her time for the last five years.

Teresa was supportive and Eliza was eternally grateful, particularly for her experience with facing adversity and making the best she could with it. They were skills Eliza would have to learn, although in some ways she already had in starting this business. If only she didn't lose it now. There was the risk. Something else she didn't have full control over as that all technically belonged to Caius.

Ahead of the meeting, she was meeting Mr. Oakwood at his office on Colston Street, which wasn't far away from where they were meeting Caius and his barrister, or so Mr. Oakwood had informed her.

On arrival, a cup of tea had been brought for her and she now sat with Mr. Oakwood while they waited. By all appearances, he was a stern man, who didn't speak much unless it was required of him, but at least he didn't treat her as if she was some fallen woman plying her trade on the streets at night.

"This will be an uncomfortable and difficult time for you," he said quietly. "Divorce cases tend to be reported minutely in the press. They may even seek to approach you, but I caution you against speaking to them. They can do damage to your case."

"I have no interest in speaking to them," she replied. "I just wish this to be over as soon as possible."

"Typically it is a protracted affair. Divorce cases are never easy and they tend to get messy. Things always do when there are emotions involved."

"Perhaps it is good then that we have had no dealings for six years. I doubt there will be any emotions involved at all. That time is passed," she drifted off. There had been a time when emotions had been extremely high, when she'd cried endlessly, and hadn't understood why this had happened. They'd been so happy, and it had all been ruined. Caius hadn't wanted to listen to her pleas, her statements that she was innocent. The proof had been overwhelming, he'd said. But how could it have been when it had never happened?

Fundamentally she hadn't understood, and still didn't, how William Castle Garrick had said such a thing. Why would he wish to do that to her? Surely he understood the implications of what he'd claimed. He'd lied about something so grave and it had destroyed her marriage. Throughout, he'd never informed her why he'd done it, had even looked at her as if she'd been disgusting.

All these things that happened to her and she hadn't understood any of it. But she clearly understood the hurt in Caius' eyes, and he'd refused to look at her as he'd commanded her to leave. The order had been given and the maids had hastily packed her belongings away in a trunk.

With a shudder, Eliza pushed away the thoughts of that day. It had been a while since she'd thought about anything that had happened back then. It served no good. Neither did thinking of the time before, or wishing things had been different. They weren't different. The accusations have been laid, and they had been believed. That was all there was to it. That was all her affection and love had been worth.

Looking up, she smiled at Mr. Oakwood. They had very little to talk about, which made it uncomfortable sitting there waiting. Why had she been so eager to arrive? Because she wanted this to be over with, and she wanted to make a good impression, but now they were stuck here with little to say. But he was very cordial, however.

"I understand the things I say to you are in confidence."

"That is correct, very much like a confessional. Anything you say to me I will keep in confidence in perpetuity."

"Mr. Oakwood," she started, "I have a business I wish to protect throughout this...palaver. It supports myself and the people who work for me. It is a small venture, and largely inconsequential. It wouldn't amount to anything substantial in Lord Warwick's eyes, but I wish to protect it."

"That may be difficult. Any contracts you've entered into, you have done in his name. That includes any leases, purchases, or any assets you hold for that matter."

"I see," she said, looking down into her teacup. "There is no way to protect it?"

"If your husband intends to dissolve it, then there's very little you can do."

"I had intended to sell down the inventory to pay for your services, Mr. Oakwood. Without the inventory, there isn't much to the company."

With a serious expression, he grew silent for a while as if he was considering her words. "In that case, it shouldn't be difficult for you to start again. Once you are divorced, then your business will be entirely under your person, but as a married woman, any activity you venture into is the domain of your husband."

"That's hardly fair as he has had no bearing or input into the business."

"No, perhaps not, but in the eyes of the law, any support he's given you has been given to this business by extension. Even if that constitutes to no support at all. The law sees him as responsible for any risk the business undertakes, hence ownership of that business, irrespective of any input he has or hasn't contributed to the business. But as you say, the company has few assets and only liabilities, then your husband might be quite happy to hand over the responsibility of those liabilities to you as part of the divorce proceedings."

Perhaps she shouldn't have mentioned it and simply pretended it didn't exist as Teresa had recommended. She wasn't sure that was possible though. At least not with the scrutiny of the press. Her activities would likely be uncovered if some reporter wanted to look into her life.

Renewed nervousness bit into her with the worry that this would destroy her business and the relationship she had with her clients and the charities she dealt with, many of whom did so because she was perceived as a moral and faultless person.

Again she sighed. None of this she had control over. It was simply a storm she had to face and afterwards she would see what was left.

Placing her tea cup down, she waited.

"I think perhaps it's time to go," Mr. Oakwood said and rose. With a smile, Eliza joined him as they walked towards the door of the silent and somber office, out past the clerk to the stairs leading down to the street. Temple was a nice part of the city, where many in the legal profession had their offices. The streets weren't as busy and everyone seemed to behave. Maybe because with so many solicitors around, everyone was on their best behavior.

It wasn't a long walk before they reached another office that was similarly sumptuous, decorated with wood paneling and marble. The name of the law firm was written with gold letters and they walked in to be greeted by a clerk. "Are you part of the Warwick party?" he asked and Mr. Oakwood nodded. "Lord Warwick is waiting in Mr. Holsten's office. You may go through at your discretion."

Nervousness bit deeply into Eliza, because he was here. It had been so very long since she'd seen him. Would he look the same?

She wasn't entirely sure why she felt so nervous, but it almost felt as if her knees wouldn't support her. It wasn't as if she was excited to see him after all this time, but she supposed she was curious. She had no idea what reception she would receive, not that she had time to think about it because they were entering the office. Perhaps harsh accusations were about to fly.

And then she saw him, standing by the window. He looked older, more mature. A man instead of the young man she had known. Some things about him seemed so very different. It had been six years, after all. She'd known throughout that time that he'd been overseas somewhere, an officer in the king's service.

No smile met her as she was so used to seeing from him as she walked into a room, but that had been so very long ago. No smiles the last few days they had been together, but before that, he would always smile when he saw her. But that man was gone, he'd left a long time ago. The man in front of her now was someone entirely different. This was Lord Warwick, and perhaps she would be better off thinking of him as an entirely different person—someone she needed to be legally separated from through this action.

"Lady Warwick," a man said and Eliza froze, not immediately understanding who they were expecting. The statement jarred into her ears. No one had ever referred to her that way, and it sounded ludicrous. Technically she was Lady Warwick until the divorce was finalized. Still, she didn't like being referred to as such—a name she didn't want or felt was warranted under the circumstances. She had always been Mrs. Hennington throughout her married life.

There was a degree of separation she required from this, rather than being seen as belonging with Caius, because they both agreed that she did not.

"We are delighted you could join us today," the man continued. Unable to help herself, her eyes darted to Caius, doubting he was in any way pleased. "Please have a seat," he said, indicating toward a chair by the table.

"I prefer Mrs. Hennington," she said. "It is how I'm known, and I prefer to continue that way." There was silence in the room and she didn't quite know how to take it. Had she just insulted him by refering to herself as a Hennington, or even by rejecting the title? It hadn't been her intention, but she didn't want to be referred to as Lady Warwick. The title seemed so wrong, and they had not been together as he'd inherited it. In fact, she hadn't even known.

"Well, I am Mr. Holsten, and I will be representing your husband through these proceedings. I understand you have engaged Mr. Oakwood to present a defense."

A defense, Eliza thought. It seems strange to have to put together a defense against divorce, but this proceeding was all about the accusation of infidelity. It wasn't simply a defense against him not wanting her as a wife, which was sheer fact. "Yes," she said and then smiled awkwardly because she didn't know what else to do. Immediately she didn't want to be there, wanted to get up and walk out of the room. All eyes were on her and she held her back straight as she walked toward the table and sat down. Mr. Oakwood sat down next to her and she was inordinately grateful he was there, even as she barely knew the man. In this room, he was all she had, and she hoped he took his position of defending her seriously.

Mr. Holsten and Caius sat down on the other side of the table. She saw him more closely now, the man she'd been so in love with. But the expression on his face was one she had seen before, but not one she was used to. That deep displeasure. If nothing else, this wasn't amusing for him either.

"Lord Warwick has agreed to cover your expenses for these proceedings," Mr. Holsten said.

Oh," Eliza replied. "That is very generous." For some reason she couldn't look at him as she said it. It was generous and part of her wanted to argue, but she knew it would financially devastate her to pay for this. It would be silly to let her pride lead her into destitution, when the offer was there and he could afford it. He had an entire estate to back him now. "Shall we proceed?" Mr. Holsten asked with curious brightness.

Chapter 7:

IN A WAY, CAIUS HAD SHUT down in a similar way as he did when battle started. The immediacy was important, and nothing else. Not his thoughts, not any emotions. It was all about the here and now.

And there she was, looking innocent and lovely. How could a visage be so deceptive? Whatever sinful life she led did not reflect on her. But she avoided his eyes, looked anywhere but at him.

Mr. Holsten spoke about the process and Caius only half listened. Truthfully, he wasn't interested in the process, only the outcome. The process, however, did guarantee that he would see her a few more times, and then they would be severed in all ways.

"There is the matter in how you wish to plead," Mr. Holsten said. He turned his attention to the other barrister. "Have you discussed this with your clients?"

"Mrs. Hennington and I have had some discussions," the man started. It offended Caius that she still used his surname, but at least she hadn't insisted on being called Lady Warwick. Perhaps she did outside these walls and only appeared modest here where she was scrutinized. "She states that she is not guilty of the charge."

Caius snorted and her eyes darted to him for a moment, then quickly away. Was that shame in her eyes?

"I understand the evidence is overwhelming. In fact, the other party to the adultery came forward and admitted it to Lord Warwick, and to several others as well."

Her head held high, she sat with a ramrod-straight back, but made no noise or expression.

"Well, that is unfortunate," Mr. Holsten said. "It could speed the proceedings up immensely if she would simply plead guilty. In this instance, we will have to hear the evidence. I take it this man is willing to testify as to what he knows?" Mr. Holsten was addressing him now. The question stumped him for a moment.

"I assume so. He has never hidden what went on. I'm sure he would be willing." Obviously, he should have asked Octavia about the whereabouts of William Castle Garrick. It simply hadn't occurred to him, because he'd thought little about the man in years.

"I believe," Eliza said and it was the first time he'd heard her voice in a long time. It was both familiar and so strange, "that he sailed for the West Indies some time ago."

"Kept in touch, did you?" he heard himself asking.

Her clear blue eye turned to him now. It was the first time she'd looked at him properly too. "No," she said and then looked away.

"That will not deter matters. We will have to get a deposition from him. It can be done, but it will slow things down. We must locate him and then we can have the local authorities act on our behalf in getting an official statement from him on this matter."

"I will make inquiries," Caius said. If she hoped that William's absence would save her, then she was wrong.

William would be found even if he had to sail over there himself.

It shouldn't prove impossible. He knew several people who he could send letters to, and if nothing else, an investigator could be hired to find the man.

"Then we must wait for this to be concluded before we can proceed with scheduling a court date. As there are no children involved, there is nothing in terms of dependents to settle. Lord Warwick has agreed to pay for the proceedings and any further issues that need to be discussed will be done as part of correspondence. So unless there is anything further to discuss..." He turned his attention to Eliza, who looked at her barrister and then shook her head.

A fury rose in Caius. An irrational part of him didn't want this to be done so clinically and coldly, wanted to rail at her and force her to admit how she'd ruined the best marriage she could ever have achieved, and to realize how utterly stupid she'd been. Because if she didn't realize, then it was on him to realize how utterly stupid he'd been in marrying her. She was living in squalor, for God's sake. How could she act like she was happy with the outcome?

Perhaps it was pride that stopped her from falling at his feet. Truthfully he didn't know if he'd have the same amount of pride when faced with such a stark reduction in circumstances. But then she had brought it on herself, and it wasn't as if her pleading was going to change anything, because he certainly wasn't going to change his mind.

"And is there anything you wish to say at this point, Lord Warwick?"

There were a million things he wished to say, in a harsh, loud voice, but he simply shook his head.

And with that, the first meeting was concluded. It would be too strong to say he'd dreaded it. Mostly he'd told himself he didn't care one whit, but it was hard to deny the anger that simmered so close to the surface. Truthfully, he'd thought himself so completely cold to her now, but the moment he saw her, it rose like a roaring beast.

As etiquette expected, he rose as she did and bowed his head. His regard for a woman did not outweigh appropriate etiquette, even for a faithless and uncouth wife.

Again he felt an irrational urge to grab her as she walked out of the room. For what reason he wasn't sure. Probably to rail at her and to release some of this anger that had been simmering inside him for years and years.

Instead, he sighed his relief when she was gone. He wasn't sure exactly how he'd expected her to react, but not as coolly as this. Maybe he'd expected tears and wailing. Melodramatics. That would not be in line with the Eliza he'd known, but it had also come out that he hadn't known her at all.

"I understand you have been supporting Mrs. Hennington throughout your separation," Mr. Holsten said.

"Yes. If living with frugality, she should have been comfortable enough."

"Any such support can cease after the divorce. As there are no children in the marriage, it can be quite a clean separation."

Caius' thoughts hadn't extended past the divorce itself, and he hadn't decided whether he wished to provide ongoing support. The angriest part of him said no, but there was a part of him that was too much of a gentleman to leave her completely in destitution, particularly as she had no standing in society anymore. No, for his own peace of mind, he would probably have to provide her with something. He could hardly have his former wife imprisoned in the workhouse, even if many felt that was what she deserved.

Right now, however, he didn't wish to speak or think about it. A simple meeting had left him feeling utterly drained. "I think we will have to leave this discussion for another day." With a nod, he left. And he knew exactly where he wanted to go. To his club that he hadn't visited in much too long. They might not even remember him at the door. They did have the best whiskey in town and right now, he needed one or two.

There was no sign of Eliza as he walked outside. Half of him had expected her to accost him as soon as he left the barrister's office, but no, she must have left. Back to Lambeth, no doubt.

Instead of taking a hack, he walked. It was some distance to St. James, but he felt he had energy to burn. As of yet, he hadn't been to Bickerley house to sort the carriage for his own use. There was much he needed to sort out with regards to Bickerley. It could be in a state for all he knew as his uncle had aged. There was also a second townhouse here in London that was his, which he needed to consider.

Eliza popped into his head for a moment, but he quickly dismissed her. There had been a time when she'd been first and foremost in his thoughts, but on the other hand, he had thought relatively little about her for many years now. It had been strange seeing her in the flesh. In his thoughts, she'd been as distant as a painting. Fixed and unmoving.

And really, where did she get the idea of pleading not guilty to the charge of adultery? Did she wish to make herself a liar to all of the world as well? If she had any sense, she would plead guilty so the whole business didn't have to be dragged out and examined for all and sundry. What in the world did she hope to achieve?

Now this would all call her character into question. That shouldn't be difficult. Her address alone was sufficient proof to many.

His return was becoming known, as would the impending divorce before long. Stories about her might come out of the woodwork. Interestingly, not to the degree that Octavia had heard anything. So either she was very discreet, or she was traveling in some truly low circles.

Another idea occurred to him, that she was some man's mistress. Fury rose again. It was bad enough that he'd been cuckolded once, but was now in the process of ridding himself of another man's mistress.

With firm strides he walked, his mind turning to mull over the kind of whiskey he wished to console himself with.

Chapter 8:

ELIZA POSITIVELY MARCHED home. Anger coursed through her body. It had been an awful meeting. Every single thing about it had felt bad. From the moment it had started, to the very end.

And the request that she plead guilty, for the purpose of making it easy for everyone. It was just too much.

Amazingly quickly she was at her door, her mind being too caught in anger to notice the streets go by. Pulling out her key from her reticule, she went inside.

"How did it go?" Teresa asked as she entered the front room.

"It was..." Eliza started, not knowing how to finish the sentence. Horrific? That might be a bit strong. "Unpleasant," she settled on. But that simply wasn't strong enough. "Well, it was an experience I should never wish to repeat. And the worst was that they wanted me to plead guilty so to expedite the process. Never mind the fact that I'm not guilty. They simply didn't care. My perspective on this simply isn't important."

Pacing around the room, she tried to dissipate some of the anger she felt.

"But he was there?"

It wasn't hard to guess who Teresa was referring to. "Yes, he was there."

"And what did he say?"

Eliza had to think about it for a moment. "I don't actually recall him saying anything." Had he even spoken? She remembered his voice, so he must have. Eliza paced some more. "I don't know," she finally said. "He has to prove my guilt, so he has to find this man who accused me, who as far as I know, isn't in England anymore."

"The case is all about adultery, so they cannot proceed without him. Provided he agrees to testify."

"I'm sure he will. He was so very keen on baseless accusations to begin with. I doubt he'll have qualms about repeating them because he must do so under oath."

"What if he cannot be found? Or is dead?"

"Perhaps he doesn't need to testify. There were enough witnesses to the accusation. Perhaps that is enough." Although she didn't know that for sure. What if William Castle Garrick couldn't be found? It was a question for her barrister. Surely the requirement wasn't dependent on the parties confessing? Was that why they wished her to plead guilty? "Poppycock," she said out loud.

"What was he like?"

"Who?" Eliza replied to the jarring question. "William the liar?"

"No, your… husband."

The question stumped her for a moment. "Well, he was older, I suppose. He must be thirty now."

"Still quite young."

"His hair was longer." And he still had that impossibly stern look on his face.

Bringing her hand up, she rubbed along her brow. It was too confronting to think about him. She hadn't in years. Not really. He'd turned into a specter for her. "He proposed to pay for the divorce proceedings."

"I suppose he can afford it. He is the one who wants a divorce. Can hardly risk it not proceedings because the woman cannot afford to hire an expensive barrister. Not many women would be in a position to do so."

"I could manage."

"We'd be much better off if he paid for it. It would mean we didn't have to strip the business down to the bare bones. That business is what will support us after he's done with you."

There was a bleak harshness in Teresa's voice, but then she did have a very poor perspective on men. And in a sense she was right. She would have very little after he was done with her. Certainly no prospects in the terms of marrying again.

"We really do need to push you to the forefront of the business," Eliza said quietly.

"I suppose there is time to do so if they are to chase this William the liar around the world. They'll want a deposition from him. Unless your husband is in too much of a hurry. Do you think there is someone he wants to marry? I understand divorces often happen when the husband wants to marry someone else."

The thought hadn't even occurred to her. But then she didn't suppose he'd been celibate the last six years. For all she knew, he could be in a relationship, one that started in the Orient, and he now wished to marry this woman.

A new level of unease washed over her. It all felt so sordid. It had been much easier with him gone, him being simply a ghost full of disdain and disapproval. Now he was real again, a real man with thoughts and wishes of his own. And clearly he wished to marry someone. An heir would also be important now that he had an estate. It would be his duty to his uncle, and Caius was always aware of his duties—except perhaps to his wife when she was falsely accused.

But from the moment he'd left, he'd diligently provided her with a stipend, as he would have seen as his duty, no matter what he thought of her. It was an action out of duty than for any affection for her. That had dried up the moment the accusation had been laid, and she'd had no recourse. How could you prove that adultery hadn't happened? There was no way to do so. It could only be denied, and it was up to others to listen or not. To not listen was what they had uniformly chosen.

"Well, I will not plead guilty simply to please others. That is a step too far. Expediency?" she said with a snort. "I am curious why I'm even needed in this process at all."

"I suppose it is possible you could refuse to participate. The trial would go ahead without you."

"That's..." Was that even possible? "They could then say anything they wanted about me."

"Which they are probably going to do irrespective of whether you are there or not. They're going to utterly defame your character."

A groan escaped her. It was all just so unpleasant.

"This change in your life is going to happen," Teresa continued. "Now it's simply a matter of making the best of it. See what's left and rebuilt. The good thing is that as a divorced woman, all the decisions you make are your own. You can enter into contracts in your own right. You can even go back to Eliza Ellerson. There is nothing to say you can't go back to using your maiden name."

For the first time, Eliza could actually see a future beyond this, and not just the overwhelming unpleasantness of the impending. "Provided our business survives."

"Well, if it doesn't, we'll rebuild. We have the skills to manage a business. We will do so again. Even if we cannot stay in educational books, we'll find something else. It will be hard, but it would be much stronger this time, and there won't be any pesky husbands in the mix."

The term 'pesky husbands' made a smile spread across Eliza's lips. Teresa had a way of seeing the potential in things, and to her, this divorce was an opportunity as well as a setback. If only Eliza had her faith, but she'd always been the more conservative one out of the two of them. She feared the impact, and worried, even as she wasn't the one who had truly seen destitution the way Teresa had when they'd first met. Maybe she feared less because she knew what it was to fear.

"There is a letter from Lord Fortescue," Teresa said. For a moment, she'd feared Teresa had said Warwick.

"Oh," Eliza said. Lord Fortescue was the man who owned the building they held the business in. They'd had some dealings recently when she'd refused to pay the rent until he fixed the leaks in the roof. It had been a negotiation. In the end, he'd capitulated and fixed the roof as she'd wished. "What could he want? We're not in arrears."

Walking back into the hallway, she saw the letter she'd missed as she'd walked in. The letter was written on fine paper, the wax sealing it closed. His seal was pressed into it. In all, she'd found him a curious man.

The seal snapped with a small crack and she opened the stiff paper and read.

"What does he want?" Teresa asked, appearing in the hallway.

"He wishes to come inspect the work done to the roof. I would have informed him if any leaks continued."

"Perhaps he simply wishes to see for himself. So he is coming to see us. Perhaps that would be a good time to talk about our continued leasing of his property. Being as he is one of *them*, he may seek to end our arrangement in light of your situation. If so, it would be good to know sooner rather than later, so we can find another building."

At times, Teresa was superbly practical, and in this instance, she was right. Lord Fortescue might object to being in business with a divorced woman. Quite a few people would, which made it all the more pressing to shed her identity as Eliza Hennington and re-establish herself as Eliza Ellerson. It wouldn't help much with the charities she was dealing with. It was likely they would take deep offense to her status as a divorced woman, but that would have to be dealt with as it cropped up.

"I guess we will just have to see what he says," Eliza said absently, tapping the envelope on her fingertips.

Chapter 9:

LITTLE HAD CHANGED at his club when Caius arrived. The people were the same, the furniture was laid out exactly as it had been.

"Jeffrey," he said as he arrived at the whiskey bar, which he'd been instrumental in installing.

"Mr. Hennington," Jeffrey said.

"Lord Warwick now, I'm afraid."

The man reddened. "My deepest apologies. I had not realized that your uncle had passed away."

"It was a recent development."

"I am sorry to hear. As always, we have an excellent selection. Is there anything I can tempt you with?"

With a sigh, Caius perused the shelves. "Perhaps the Brenock Golden."

"Excellent choice," the man said, exactly as he always had years earlier. It was nice that some things never changed.

The liquid really was golden, like captured sunlight. After the afternoon he'd had, he could use a little brightness. It had all felt very bleak. Eliza had looked exactly the same. The years had not worn her in the least. If she led a disreputable lifestyle, it certainly didn't show on her. There was always something a bit lovely about her, dreamy, but looks were deceiving, and he knew that more than most.

This was all so very sordid. But here was joy in a small glass, and he lifted it to his mouth.

"Hennington," someone said, clapping him on the back so the whiskey spilt. Caius closed his eyes. With another deep breath, he ignored the man and drank. It was rude, but so was approaching a man in mid-appreciation.

The whiskey coated his mouth and tongue, then the smooth burn as it went down. Countryside, rough hills and ocean gales. Sometimes the roughness of the British countryside was captured perfectly. It wasn't all gentle hills and meandering dairy cows. Whiskey was made in the wilder parts of the country.

Gently, he put the glass down. Yes, he'd made a good choice with that one. Now to the intruder. "Rawley," he said, turning to the man waiting expectantly, having just been ignored. "How are you these days?" The man's hairline wasn't what it had been. They had known each other at Oxford.

"Good, good," he said. "I understand you have been fortunate and come into a title. Congratulations, old man."

Henry Rawley would stubbornly be waiting for his title for a long time. His father had married young and had a good few decades to go yet. Henry might well be in his fifties before he received his title and estate. It made him not optimally appealing on the marriage market, but there would be some families with foresight who would be happy to wait. Perhaps it had happened already, but the man had that bachelor sense about him. The gleam of youthful mischief in his eyes. Married men lost that. Not all of them as there were some who still wanted to roam London's streets with their fellow miscreants.

"I am so pleased you have returned from the wilds," Rawley said. "You must join us tonight."

Caius smiled. No, he wouldn't be roaming the establishments of London with the youthful miscreants. "I'm afraid I have plans."

"Of course," Rawley said, his smile not budging. "And how is your brother?"

"Good."

"Still not married?"

"No, not yet.

"Getting a bit long in the tooth."

"Aren't we all."

"I suppose with that awful business, it might have put him off."

By the awful business, he meant the deceptive Eliza. There was an awkward silence. The man was curious about what he was going to do about her now. They all were. It must have been the topic on every gossiping tongue who was familiar with his affairs. Equally, all would be judging him for having made such an atrocious choice in bride. They had a point. For generally being able to make good decisions, he'd made an awful one with regards to the most important of his life.

"Yes, perhaps," Caius finally said. This divorce would be quite closely followed—maybe to the point where he had to stay clear of the club for a while. Some, like Rawley, didn't have the sense to leave things be when appropriate.

"The lady in question hasn't been seen, I have to say," Rawley continued. "Neither has the Lancelot in this case." Rawley was clearly pressing for information. "Makes one wonder if they absconded together, living somewhere in sinful bliss."

Clearly, Rawley had no idea about William Castle Garrick's whereabouts, nor Eliza's—although he could imagine Rawley trying to seduce her if he did know. Men like him might be why she stayed away from this society. Unless some cad just like him had her hidden away somewhere. A wave of nausea assaulted him. If so, it wasn't William Castle Garrick, because according to Eliza, he had absconded to the West Indies.

How had she known this if Rawley didn't know? Had they met after they'd been uncovered and he'd confessed his plans to leave her behind? Had it broken her heart?

Where had that thought come from? She deserved it for being so utterly stupid if that was the case.

Another thought occurred to him. Surely it couldn't be a ruse—her trying to deflect attention away from them, when they were hidden away in Lambeth. It would be an untruth to say she didn't lie. That had certainly been uncovered. No, he needed an impartial opinion on this.

"Have you seen Sommerset lately?" Caius asked.

"I saw him earlier this evening, actually. He might still be around."

"Right," Caius said absently. "It was good to see you," he said, slapping the man on the shoulder.

"About tonight," Rawley said as he walked away, but Caius ignored him, not understanding why he'd want his company on an evening in the gutter. It wasn't as though they'd spent any length of time together since Oxford.

"Some other time," Caius called and turned his attention to the search for Sommerset. The man was found in the smoking room, reading the paper. Caius took the empty chair opposite the small table and the man folded his paper down and then looked surprised.

"There is a face I haven't seen for some time. Hennington, or rather Lord Warwick now, I presume. I was sorry to hear about your uncle."

"Yes, we were all devastated. Now you have properties in the West Indies, do you not?"

"Yes, Jamaica."

"I am trying to track someone who went and I was wondering if you've heard of him."

"Oh?"

"William Castle Garrick."

The man leant his head back on the chair as if thinking. "I have heard the name. Can't place it, though. In all honesty I don't know the society there all that well. I only visit briefly and usually for a specific reason. Although I do know someone who might know more."

"Right. In that case, an introduction would be much appreciated."

"A Mrs. Moore. She has recently returned and is more familiar with the people coming and going. That is for Jamaica, mind you. There is more to the West Indies. Some real hideaway places for people who don't want to be found. It can be impossible to track someone who doesn't want to be found."

"I doubt that is the case here," Caius said. William Castle Garrick wasn't a solitary man. Society would draw him. The man was too fond of a party, and too much a cad to be worried about a bit of scandal. "No, I might have to call on this Mrs. Moore, if that is not too much of a bother."

"I will let her know to expect you. I'll have my man send over her address. Nice woman, but quite the gossip."

"I believe I have met the type before," Caius stated.

"How is your father?"

"Good. He is aging."

"Aren't we all," Sommerset said with a huff. "It would be good to see him once in a while."

"He seems to like it at Denham too much these days."

"Well, when you see him, tell him he's a little too young to embrace his dotage just yet."

A smile spread across Caius' lips, because his father wouldn't like the comment at all, which was the reason Sommerset was saying it. Getting too comfortable on one's estate simply wasn't allowed. If one had to suffer the tribulations of London, they all should.

"I will certainly pass that on," Caius said as he rose. "And I will call on Mrs. Moore. Thank you for the recommendation." Finding William was important for the trial. His deposition would cut any counter-arguments that Eliza could come with. Third-party observers to an accusation didn't have the weight of a confession from one of the parties to the actual adultery.

During their meeting, he'd gotten little understanding of the strategies Eliza sought to employ. Her face had reddened as Mr. Holsten had suggested she plead guilty. She certainly hadn't liked that. Her emotions were written on her face. Anger. Disgust. Was it not herself she should be angry and disgusted with, rather than the request that she own her actions?

Chapter 10:

IT WAS ALWAYS A BUSY day when an order needed to go out. Normally, it wasn't quite so satisfying to see the inventory decreasing, but it had a certain satisfaction right now, because it would do her good in the divorce. As was their plan, they would reduce the inventory as much as possible. Although she was still quite taken by the idea of not mentioning the business at all, even as she knew it was a childish impulse. Such actions never worked in the long run. She hadn't been a child for a long time, who would ignore their problems in the hope that they would simply disappear.

Someone clearing their throat drew her attention, and to her surprise, she turned to see Lord Fortescue, the owner of the building they were occupying. She'd only met the man once and their dealings had been contentious. After suffering consistent leaks in the roof, she'd refused to pay the rent until they were fixed. To her amazement, he'd fixed the roof.

"Lord Fortescue," she said, putting her inventory records to side and walked toward him. "To what do we owe the pleasure? I hope nothing is wrong," she said, but with each step, she started to fear that something was very wrong—that he'd heard of the impending divorce and was about to throw her out in disgust of his perception of her character.

"I was simply passing and thought I would come see how you are. I trust the repairs have been completed to your satisfaction."

"Yes, wholly. We have no leaks whatsoever, I am pleased to report." Looking back, she felt a little ashamed how forthright she'd been, demanding he fix the roof. "Our inventory has been quite safe. I cannot thank you enough."

"It is my pleasure." His eyes searched the large space as if he hadn't seen it before. There was no doubt he was a handsome man. Light brown, wavy hair. Imposing in his height. Green eyes, she saw when he turned to her, and she hoped he hadn't just caught her admiring him. "It is an interesting little business you have here. It is an unusual step for a woman such as yourself."

Her smile faltered slightly. From his perspective, it probably was an unusual step for a married woman of the social standing her husband had. "There was a great need for it, I found. One I couldn't look past. And I find I need something to occupy my thoughts."

"An admirable quality."

Biting her lips together, she considered what to do, because a woman such as herself, as he saw her, wasn't entirely accurate. "There is an issue I wish to discuss with you, and it is pertinent to this business."

"I see," he said.

Nerves clenched her stomach as he turned his attention to her. It had been a long time since a man had particularly paid attention to her, and she didn't quite know how to receive it. Perhaps it was simply that he was such a handsome man.

"As I am sure this business alludes, the standing between myself and my husband isn't entirely... optimal."

Looking around she tried to formulate her words, but he beat her to it. "Hence you need this business to support yourself?" There was concern in his voice. How could he be so thoughtful? Although that thoughtfulness might not continue once he found out her true situation.

"No, not entirely. The need I spoke about drove me to start this business. Saying that, I may need it to support me, presently. You see, my husband has returned from many years overseas and he wishes not to continue with this... less than optimal marriage. It is fair to say we cannot reconcile."

He listened without interrupting and remained silent.

Clearing her throat, she continued. "So there is likely to be a bit of unpleasantness, including..." Now she wished she hadn't embarked on this at all, but it had to be done. If he was going to throw her out, it would be good to know so ahead of time, so she could make alternative arrangements. "...including some substantial detriment to my character."

"I don't understand."

Perhaps she was being too delicate in her words. "He is divorcing me."

"Oh," he said, his eyes looking around the space again as if reassessing it.

"So in the not-too-distant future, you will be renting this space to a divorced woman."

"Will this not amount to a detriment to the business as well?"

It wasn't the question she'd expected. "Yes, it might do. We are actively promoting my business partner, Teresa Broadman, to take a more prominent role in the company."

Stepping around with his hands clasped behind his back, he seemed to consider his words. His evaluation of her was about to be announced, and she felt extraordinarily nervous. For some reason, she didn't wish him to have a bad opinion about her. "I see," he finally said. "I can see why this business has become so important for you."

"I would lie if I said that wasn't so."

"There will be considerable scandal with divorce."

"So I understand."

"You are aware that any contracts you've entered into are in the name of your husband, including the lease for this space. The decisions over them are likely to flow to him as part of a divorce."

For this she didn't have a ready response. Yes, she was aware, but she didn't entirely understand what the implications were. Her understanding of Caius had been that he wasn't a vindictive man, but how could she say that for sure? "Yes, some preparations are needed. It is highly unlikely he will have any interest in this business. I understand he has a substantial estate to concern himself with."

"It is a precarious position you are in, Mrs. Hennington."

"Yes, unfortunately. I am making whatever preparations I can to minimize any disruption."

"In fact, he could close this business down in a moment and there would be nothing you can do about it."

Was she being hopeful that Caius would wish to preserve her livelihood? He was so very angry with her and it had been apparent when they'd met in that barrister's office.

"I assume that adultery will be the charge he will use to affect this divorce."

"Yes," she said with a snort.

"It is an unfair situation when a man deserts a woman and then blames her for being disloyal."

"I assure you, while there was an accusation, I profess no guilt." Her words were strong, her anger still there for the barrister's insistence that she plead guilty.

"It is hard to have an upper hand in a situation like this. They will seek to prove your guilt. For them it is imperative to. From your perspective, it is hard to fight such a charge. Your husband must feel he has stable grounds for such a charge."

"Well, yes, he does, but that does not make it true."

"I'm not really sure it matters if it's true or not. It only matters what he can convince the court of. Do you think he will be able to?"

"I am sure he can, although he wishes for me to make the whole affair much easier for everyone by pleading guilty. Then they won't have to prove anything." Whereas now they had to get a deposition from the Caribbean, which would take time and effort, and it was their just desserts that they had to work hard to convince a court of this fallacy. But with William Castle Garrick's declarations of her guilt, there would be little to do.

And she really shouldn't be having this conversation with her landlord, but she wished to establish an understanding between them.

"Now that is something," he said.

"What is?"

"A man who wishes to go through the embarrassment and expense of seeking a divorce will find a way of attaining it."

"No doubt," she agreed. Courts cared little of aggrieved females. That had been shown as true more than a few times.

"You do have some bargaining power if they wish for an easy and expedient way through your profession of guilt."

"Are you saying I should bargain my guilt?"

"I would. If they are to prove it anyway, then bargain what you can for it. If there is something you wish to keep, now is the time to bargain."

"But I am not guilty."

"Does it matter?" he asked. "At times, it is more important to make the best of a situation—if one has something to lose. Pride is but pride."

For a moment, she was stumped. It was a very practical approach he proposed. He was right that fighting for her pride was a losing battle, and she should use the one bargaining tool to achieve what she needed to achieve. Her pride wasn't paramount.

"I suppose we will see who I end up holding a lease with—you or your husband?" With a raised eyebrow, he smiled. "Good day, Mrs. Hennington. I am pleased the repairs have been satisfactory."

With a nod, he started walking away.

"Lord Fortescue," she called to him, "would you keep the lease with a divorced woman?"

Stopping, he turned. "I think I know what I need to know of your character," he replied. For some reason, she blushed. "And you do pay your rent on time, when you feel I am providing a premise up to your standards. Good luck with your divorce. Through some things we can only fare as best as we can. I will not end the lease because you are divorced."

It was very understanding of him and her opinion of him rose enormously. And now she was left considering his advice. Bargain the business for her guilt. It would certainly assure the best possible outcome for her, although it would hurt her pride to admit guilt to something she was fundamentally not guilty of. Even in the years of her husband's absence, she had never strayed. It hadn't been something she'd sought, but she also recognized it was pride that had driven her there too.

Chapter 11:

CAIUS COULDN'T DETERMINE whether he hated or loved being back in London. Being at Denham Hall and dealing with his family all day was too much to bear, so he preferred being in London, but at times, he wished he was anywhere but back in England. Equally, he hadn't rushed to Bickerley, because when he took possession of it, it would no longer be his uncle's, but his. It had a certain finality he'd been putting off. It wasn't as if he was scared of it, because being a military man, he knew what it was to fear. No, it was more the avoidance of emotion and the realization that things truly had changed.

Perhaps there was only so much change one could handle at one time. Right now, the most pressing was the dissolution of his marriage. Something else necessary, but not something he was relishing.

In front of him sat the letter asking Mrs. Moore if he could come see her with regards to the whereabouts of William Castle Garrick. He was just about to have it mailed to her. It may well be that she knew exactly where he was and how he could be reached. William did tend to make himself known.

The divorce couldn't really proceed until this was done, so he had better get on with it. The letter fit into the envelope perfectly and he lit a candle to melt the ruby red wax to seal it. As of yet, he didn't have the stamp of Lord Warwick, so he used his old one that had traveled the whole of the world with him.

Mr. Jones appeared at the door, which he only did if something urgently needed his attention. "What is it?" Caius asked.

"You have a visitor?"

"Oh?" It was perhaps not surprising that old acquaintances called. News was getting around regarding his return.

"A Mrs. Henningon, it seems," Jones said.

The name had Caius blinking for a moment. Eliza was here? For what purpose? Mortifying scenes tumbled through his mind. Surely she wasn't going to plead for him not to go through with the divorce, or in any way suggest they should reconcile? That would be preposterous.

In all honesty, he just didn't know the lengths she would stoop to, or why she was there. Perhaps he should turn her away to spare them both a highly embarrassing encounter. But no, if she needed to understand something, it was better to reach that understanding sooner rather than later. "Well, I suppose you had better show her in."

The man's expressions were hard to make out, but Caius instinctively knew that Jones was curious. They didn't have the kind of relationship where they talked about personal matters. Their relationship was exclusively practical in nature, and they both preferred it that way. "In the parlor?"

"No, bring her here. And take this letter to the post as soon as you can."

In no way did he want this to come across as a social call. Whatever motive she had for being there, he wished to disabuse her of them if required.

A certain discomfort assaulted him as Jones left to retrieve her. Meeting at the legal office had provided little opportunity to talk, and he'd been happy that way. No, anything was on the cards.

And then she appeared, looking similar to how he remembered her from his barrister's office. During his time in the Orient, he'd forbidden himself to think about her at all, and that had served him rather well. There was no point dwelling on the past, or on what she'd done.

"Eliza," he said as she walked into the room, wearing a cream and pink dress. There had always been something of a dreamy quality to her. The dress seemed to match her complexion, creamy with pink cheeks. It appeared she had walked here. Could she not afford a hack to convey her? Perhaps she was trying to make herself look pitiable. "What can I do for you?" In no way did he infuse any real curiosity or warmth into his tone. In truth, there was little he wished to do for her. He certainly wasn't going to insist this was a pleasure, because it really wasn't.

"How are you?"

"Is this a social call?" he asked, showing a degree of annoyance.

"No, I'm afraid not."

Taking his seat, he weaved his fingers together, a little angry with himself for having risen as she walked in. She didn't deserve the respect, but the politeness was ingrained. Without speaking, he waited for her to state her business.

"The other day, your advisor seemed to suggest that it would make everything easier if I plead guilty to whatever charges put against me during the divorce trial."

"By whatever charges, you mean adultery."

A tight smile formed on her lips, but she didn't answer.

"Yes, it could circumvent the need to establish the validity of the accusation."

"I understand that could be difficult and time-consuming as the accuser is on the other side of the world."

"It would help having his input, but it's not necessary. There were sufficient witnesses who can testify as to what happened."

Where was she going with this? She was clearly here to discuss the divorce.

"It would be a great deal of trouble and would ensnare your family into this sordid matter."

"What is your point, Eliza?" he said, losing his patience.

"Only that I am agreeable to making this process easier for all involved by pleading guilty, but I will do so under one condition."

His eyebrows rose, not sure if he should laugh or be offended by this. Not for the first time, it occurred to him that he didn't really know her as he'd thought he had. Her persona, her façade, had all been a lie. "And what is the condition you stipulate."

"I have a small business. One that is of no consequence to you. I simply wish for you to leave it intact, and in my care from now and after the divorce."

"A small business?" he said with confusion. "What business is that?"

"I create and print educational material for charities."

The answer was not what he expected. "And that is your one and only stipulation?" A business. He could hardly see it. Well, she had always liked drawing, he supposed.

"Yes, that is my only stipulation. The divorce will conclude with the transfer of ownership of all assets, contracts, and liabilities related to this business to me. And that includes any products related to the business that I have."

Tapping his thumbs together, he tried to think through any way she might be trying to dupe him through this action. "And what assets are involved with this business?" The only thing he could think of was property of his estate which she had drawn into the business. It wasn't the townhouse, because there had been no sight of her there when he'd arrived, and the servants had been queried. She hadn't involved herself with them or the house in any way.

"Only printed material we have created."

"Alright, fine. I agree."

The ghost of a smile flittered across her lips. "Good, right. Then you can depend on my guilt," she said tartly.

"I will, of course, be very disappointed if you don't carry through with your end of the bargain."

"I certainly will."

"I have by nature become quite suspicious of your vows."

"Then you will be pleasantly surprised," she stated. "But Mr. Holsten will be very disappointed in me if I don't get this bargain in writing, and the agreement to transfer the business and anything pertaining to it into my ownership."

If this was some kind of ruse, it may be worth it for an expedient divorce trial. It would make things easier, especially if Mr. Castle Garrick's continued absence proved to be a problem. He was still suspicious. "Well, I am pleased you have decided to be amiable with regards to this. I don't think either of us wants a drawn-out and protracted affair."

"Have a signed agreement sent to Mr. Holsten, and then you simply have to inform us when the trial is. I will be there. Good day."

Her goodbye greeting was curt. It seemed she had no other business she wished to discuss and had obviously gotten what she wanted. She was gone before his bow was complete. Clearly not keen to linger in his company.

Slowly, he sat down again, not entirely sure what he'd just agreed to. A business. It wasn't what he'd expected. Charity work. Well, that did sound kind of like her. And this was the one thing she wanted from this marriage, because it was the only thing she bargained for. It may well be that he would have made more concessions for her guilty pleas, but she had settled for the 'inconsequential' business she had built.

Well, it was done now. He had agreed, and he would keep that bargain no matter what it turned out to involve.

Maybe he didn't need to trace Mr. Castle Garrick now, as it was likely to greatly increase the duration of this divorce. "Mr. Jones?"

Jones appeared. "I just showed her out."

"Did you mail the letter I gave you?"

"Yes, it has gone."

Damn, he said silently. Involving this woman might be entirely unnecessary, but the letter had gone, and it wasn't worth chasing it down. "Right, thank you," he said absently.

Chapter 12:

IN HIS DRESSING ROBE, Caius sat at the desk in his bedroom and tapped his finger on the polished mahogany. The events of the day before kept returning to his mind—his agreement to sign over the business Eliza had built to her. It was the fact that she had built a business that astounded him. He would never have guessed it. Equally interesting was her single-minded determination to protect it.

From her perspective, she saw it as a source of income, which was understandable. As a divorced woman, an income was crucial, so it was hardly surprising she'd sought to secure it. Still, she had said it was inconsequential.

What kind of business was it? According to her own words, it provided educational material to charities. What could that possibly mean?

Rising, he walked to the door in swift strides. "Jones!" he called. It took some moments before the man appeared.

"What do you want?"

The man's manners were something Caius had given up on. Jones was never going to be the mild-mannered servant, but he was supremely good at organizing. The man could orchestrate an invasion of Scotland if it should prove necessary. "There is a business producing educational material for charities. Probably situated in Lambeth or thereabouts. Could you be so kind as to find it."

"You have a name for this business?"

"No, but Mrs. Hennington is the proprietress. Maybe if you ask around, someone thereabouts will know of her."

"You have the address of her rooms. I could simply follow her."

The statement gave him pause. That sounded a little too shifty. "If you must," he finally conceded. "But don't be seen." The last thing Caius wanted was Eliza marching over here accusing him of having her followed. A practice not unknown in divorce cases, truth be told. Although hardly necessary as she was to plead guilty.

So it seemed she was ready to acknowledge what she'd done. No doubt, she would be asked to provide details in court with regards to it, and Caius wasn't sure he wanted to know. Hearing it might bring back all the unpleasantness he'd been embroiled in at the time. It certainly wouldn't be delightful to have those details publicized in every newspaper in the country.

Jones left, no doubt delighted in a bit of reconnaissance.

Feeling restless, Caius returned to his desk and sat down. He should probably dress, but there was no real hurry. Nothing urgent was pressing on him, particularly now that Eliza had agreed to plead guilty. Perhaps her conscience had held sway on her. But the idea that she traded this plea for her business still sat with him. Perhaps it was a sensible choice for her.

Which now left him with the decision of how much to provide for her in ongoing support after the divorce. Technically, he didn't need to, and it could even be unnecessary that he do so if this business supported her. There were just so many unsettled questions. Not to mention having to deal with Bickerley, which he needed to do.

With a sigh, his eyes perused the desk, seeking something here that needed him. No, he had to plan a trip to Bickerley and pulled over a fresh piece of paper with his Hennington letterhead. Another thing to do was to order new letterhead.

He addressed the letter to his late uncle's butler, informing the man to expect him in a few days' time. What he would find at Bickerley, he had no idea. His uncle could have let things go to rack and ruin in his last years. It wasn't unheard of with elderly estate owners. His uncle had always been a strong, stout man, but age had a way of undoing strength. As for himself, he couldn't imagine old age, or his life at his uncle's age. It would clearly be at Bickerley too. Perhaps he would never get to such advanced years.

A wife and children by his side was something else he couldn't imagine. There had been a time when he'd seen his future with Eliza, but with her betrayal, he'd given up on the idea entirely. And he didn't relish the thought of choosing another bride. Such duties would have to wait until after the divorce was settled. Being titled with good prospects, it wouldn't be too difficult. And at this point, he was looking for good character rather than someone who inflamed him.

Abandoning the desk, he dressed and checked the weather outside. Gray skies with a potential of rain, he would guess. The paper would be waiting for him downstairs and he would read it with his breakfast. That was really how far his plans went. Perhaps he should have the Bickerley accounts sent to him so he could study them before journeying there.

Breakfast was a silent affair in an empty room, the turning of the newspaper pages sounding stark as it echoed off the walls. London went about its business with misdeeds, financial gains and losses and whatever scandal was the talk of the town. It would be him soon enough. With Eliza pleading guilty, he could well be painted as the pitiable wronged party. It was true, but he didn't like the idea of being pitied. It had driven him from England in the first place.

But one could never truly escape anything. All his problems had simply waited patiently for him to return. At least he was less heated about it all now.

Jones' steps were heard. That didn't take long, Caius conceded. The man appeared at the door. "My lord," he said with a nod. It still sounded wrong, his title coming from Jones, but it was still the correct way of addressing him.

"You found it."

"I did. Babbling Brook Educational Books it is called. It is located in a warehouse on Coldwell Street."

"A warehouse?"

"Yes."

That was more than some small parlor business. "A whole warehouse?"

"Yes."

Again he was astonished that Eliza would do such a thing. And Babbling Brook. That had been her name for the stream nearby the house she'd grown up in. He didn't recall the instance of her mentioning it, but he still knew of it. It must have been something she'd mentioned at some point, a fact that had stuck in his head without him being aware of it until it was now mentioned.

"Deliveries come, deliveries go," Jones continued.

"Deliveries," Caius repeated absently. "This is a proper business."

"I would say so."

"It would not be referred to as inconsequential?"

"I suppose that depends on the context."

Caius had to concede the point. From some perspectives, it could be perceived as inconsequential. Eliza had clearly assigned that perspective to him. Still, it was deceptive. Clearly she feared him taking her business away from her. It could still be seen as dishonest misrepresenting the size of the business. "Coldwell Street, you said?"

"Yes, my lord."

It may be that he needed to see this for himself to get a true understanding of how severely she'd deceived him. Not that he would have taken the business away from her if she'd been honest, but it was the deception that grated.

"My coat, I think."

"You wish me to bring the carriage?"

"No, I shall walk." Some exercise would do him well. In his new life, there was too much sitting in comfortable rooms for his liking.

Coat donned, he left his townhouse and walked down toward Parliament and then across the Thames. Such a short distance, but a distinct change in neighborhood. Gone were the fine carriages and silk dressed ladies, replaced with working men and carts. The streets were meaner and dirtier, people going about their business as quickly as possible. This was a place of business and poverty.

It didn't take long to find Coldwell Street, although he had to ask where the warehouse housing books was from the street vendors, who eventually set him right. No signage was written on the building, which suggested it was rented rather than owned. Eliza had said the business had no assets other than the printed books, so the premises were leased, but it was a large warehouse, which made him question if this really was for charities. The charitable businesses he'd known of were small things, done to pass spare time, but this was not that.

For a while, he stood there, considering what to do. Should he confront her about her lies? Technically, they hadn't been lies, only bending of the truth. So why was he upset? Because she'd aimed to deceive him once again.

As he watched, Eliza opening a door, ushering a child out. Caius stared. There was a child? Blood coursed through his body and he had to quell the rage rising sharply. This was more than a simple deception. This was... extraordinary. Was this his child she was hiding from him?

"Eliza!" he called, his voice booming across the street, sharply drawing her attention. Was that fear of being uncovered in her lies that he saw on her face? "A word!"

Chapter 13:

WITH POWERFUL STRIDES, Caius walked toward her, carts and people barely getting out of his way. How was he here? What was he doing here?

"Lord Warwick?" she said as he approached, a look on his face she hadn't seen for quite a while.

"There is a child. You've hidden a child from me?"

"I'm sorry?"

"You're sorry! Is there no end to your deception?"

"Rosie, please go back inside for a moment," she said without her eyes leaving him, because at the moment, she wasn't entirely sure she trusted him, or anything related to this extraordinary behavior. Clearly he was accusing her of something. "Go sit with Mr. Henry, and I will come to you in a minute." Breaking her gaze away, she looked and smiled at the girl who was clearly distressed. The girl ran off. "I demand in the future that any correspondence between us be done through our solicitors."

"Oh, you don't wish to admit your deception while looking in my eyes?"

"What deception?" she said harshly.

"The child. You think it would not be something I needed to know?"

"I don't understand."

"My child."

It dawned on her the mistake he was clearly making. "No, you misunderstand." This felt a little like negotiating with a raging bull. His face was colored with anger and his gaze piercing. How dare he come here and make fallacious accusations? "Simply because you see me walking with a child does not justify your nonsensical accusations?"

"You deny it?"

"Deny what exactly?"

"That you carried a child in secret."

"That child is eight. I think you would have noticed if I was nursing a child when we married." Her voice was rising and she was conscious that people were noticing them quarrel in the street like some uncouth pair.

"So you had the child before we married and then hid it. There's—"

"There has to be an end to your ridiculous accusations!" she said sharply. "The child is not mine."

He snorted, clearly not believing her. "Good day, sir."

"My lord," he said sharply, correcting her address.

"Why don't you bring up my lack of proper respect during the court case," she bit sharply. "Now leave me be, you ridiculous man."

Eliza marched off, unsure if he followed her. This was embarrassing and completely unjustified. Clearly he had an opinion of her that assumed she was capable of anything. Abruptly, she stopped. Rosie was still inside the warehouse and she couldn't walk off without her.

Turning, she walked back, Caius still staring at her. With harsh strides, she walked back.

"Are you claiming this is not your child?" he asked.

When had he become so utterly unreasonable? "That dog, that lamp post and that cart are not mine either, even as they are around me right now. Now please leave."

Moving past him, she walked toward the door to the warehouse.

"But this is your warehouse."

She paused. "It is a warehouse I lease."

"For the completely inconsequential business."

"As I told you, I print and sell books for charities. Everything I said was true."

"You did not convey the scale of things."

Letting go of the door handle, she walked back to him. "Do you wish to renege on our bargain so you can take my business?"

There was a faltering in his eyes. An uncertainty. "No," he said.

"Good. Now please leave, you have done quite enough to terrify small children today. And as I said, if you have any other baseless accusations, please deliver them to my solicitor. Good day."

With that, she turned and walked to the door again, disappearing inside without a look back. Away from sight, she stopped. Her whole body shook, her hands. Her heart beat and tears were threatening. Why was dealing with him so hard? And why did she deserve such disrespect? To come and fling idiotic accusation at her, in the street, where anyone could have observed it.

Taking a deep breath, she wiped her fingers over her eyes. Things were difficult enough without his clear stupidity and carelessness. Why in the world would he jump to the conclusion that Rosie was her child and that she had hidden her from him? It was the most outlandish accusation, and truly it wasn't in character for him. Who would jump to such a conclusion based on her exiting a door with a child?

Perhaps his time in the Far East had destroyed his nerves, or sense. Or he was utterly mad. If the divorce failed to proceed with her guilty plea of adultery, she could start building a case for insanity. Unfortunately, it was not a recognized cause for divorce.

"Rosie?" she called and the girl appeared, clearly scared and uncertain.

"He is gone."

"Who is he?" Rosie asked.

"That is my former husband. He's not right in the head, but I told him quite clearly not to come again." She tried to smile, but it probably looked more like a grimace. "What do you think about me calling a hack to take us home?"

The girl nodded, clearly worried that man was still out there somewhere. Again, Eliza cursed Caius for being such a stupid brute.

Mr. Henry appeared. "What's this nonsense?" he said.

"Nothing. Could you be so kind as to call us a hack, Mr. Henry?"

The man nodded and walked out the door.

"That man is not a threat," Eliza said. "Just accusations. He's very good at those, but you don't need to fear him."

"If he comes around again, I'll kick him in the shins."

"And he'd deserve it."

Mr. Henry returned and held the door open for them. A hack waited outside and Eliza helped Rosie get in before doing so herself. Once inside, she looked out to see if Caius was still there, but he appeared to have gone.

Well, this had certainly been a disturbing episode in the queasy saga that was their marriage. For all the damage it would do, it was certainly good to put an end to the miserable union.

It didn't take them long to get home and Rosie rushed inside while she paid the driver. Finally closing the door behind her as she walked inside.

"What's this?" Teresa asked, coming into the small hallway. "What man?"

"Lord Warwick paid a visit today." Eliza really didn't want to talk about this right now, but she understood Teresa's concern when her child had been frightened.

"And he was yelling at you?"

"It seemed he was under the impression that Rosie was my child and I had hidden her from him."

With a frown, Teresa crossed her arms. "I suppose you corrected his assumption."

"I did." Eliza walked past into the parlor and sighed heavily as she sat down.

Teresa followed, walking slowly into the room until she stood in the middle. "That is quite irrational," she said. "What an extraordinary accusation."

"I know," Eliza said.

"Is he mad?"

Eliza shrugged. "He's been a soldier for years. Perhaps he's turned mad."

"Still, that's... extraordinary. He was just yelling at you on the street? It sounds unhinged."

Well, it had been unhinged. "I can't have him coming around and scaring the children. I told him he could only correspond through solicitors in the future."

Teresa stroked her hand down her mouth. "You don't think he would be violent?"

"No, I cannot see it." At no point had she ever seen him lose control of himself and be violent, but then he had been a soldier. "We will divorce and that will be the end of it. I think in preparation, we should go around all the charities, by we, I mean you, and say that I am stepping away from my participation in the company."

"But you are not."

"Technically through the trial, I will be. But it is better that you are the person they see as the head of the company now." It was a stretching of the truth, just like Caius had accused her of, but it was necessary to protect the company. How could that be a bad thing? What was the alternative, to let the company sink along with her reputation? No, they had to twist things to appear in a better light.

Perhaps his accusation was true in that she had twisted things, used certain words to make it appear as if her company was smaller than it really was. In light of his accusation of adultery, which was plain untruth, it was a small infraction. Everyone else's lies were forcing her to take steps to protect what was hers. He could make accusations of it if he wanted, but she could not regret it. And he'd stated he would not undo the bargain, so nothing was lost.

Still, she didn't like being accused of omitting the truth. In many ways, she was guilty of it, even if being perceived of much worse offenses. Clearly he thought her a woman who would hide a child. First his child, then that had shifted to a child before their marriage. He had known she was chaste on their wedding night. Men knew such things, apparently. But all those things had gone out the window and he'd resorted to boundless accusations. Perhaps he was mad.

Chapter 14:

THE CARRIAGE STEADILY made its way to Devon. The roads were good, but Caius' head ached with every slight bump and movement. Pain he deserved for being such an idiot the day before. To then go compound the issue by drinking heavily to bury how disappointed he was in himself.

For the life of him, he couldn't understand why he'd so utterly flown off the handle, and had irrationally accused her of misdeeds based on no facts whatsoever. Eliza had said so as well and had clearly dismissed him.

He didn't dare guess what her opinion was of him right then. To escape it all, he was doing what he'd been putting off for quite some time, going to survey Bickerley.

Eliza had to think he was touched in the head, and he had a hard time justifying himself. Why would he do such a thing? It was completely out of his character. Jumping to conclusions wasn't something he engaged in. He'd be long dead on the battlefield if he'd engaged in such silliness, but the moment he'd seen her with that child, his heart had stopped, along with his brain.

Again he winced thinking back on it. It was rare that his own self was unfathomable to him, but this was one such occasion.

Leaning his head back, he let the movement of the carriage lull him. There was nothing he could do to undo the day before, so he simply had to accept it.

In time, he arrived at Bickerley, the journey time short because of the train that ran toward this part of the country now. They truly were marvelous inventions, because this journey would have taken days before.

The stately house appeared in view, but his heart didn't soar at the sight like it normally had the times he'd come here as a youth. He still mourned his uncle and taking his place wasn't a joy. At the same time, he felt guilty for not having been there for his uncle in the last six years. As of yet, he didn't know if his uncle had truly needed him, but perhaps that was what he feared learning.

The house itself was built of stone, ornate stonework above the windows, and a Palladian portico at the entrance. It was a lovely house. Three stories in height and rectangular in shape. The gravel was bare in spots, so that was one task that needed doing. Perhaps he needed to prepare an actual list.

"Good evening, Mr. Simmons," he said to the elderly man who came out to greet him. "I trust you were aware of my arrival."

"Yes, welcome. Thank you for letting us know you were coming."

Caius didn't doubt the house had been scrubbed from top to bottom in preparation for the new owner. It was largely unnecessary, but he'd learned not to interfere with matters of the house. Such things were best left to whatever Mr. Simmons felt was best.

The house was familiar inside, wood paneling and carpeted floors. The furniture was the same, old and comfortable. Nothing much had changed in this house for a long time. Perhaps some of the furniture needed reupholstering, but that wasn't urgent. More important was to ensure the lands were productive. Although when a wife came along, the inside of the house should be addressed.

It was still difficult to imagine a wife of his installed in this house. Eliza fleeted into mind. That was how he'd always seen the topic, and he'd given it little thought since. Perhaps when the divorce was final and he started meeting eligible young ladies, he could finally imagine someone else in her stead.

Slowly he wandered around the house, reaching the library where his uncle had liked to sit in the evenings by the fire. His chair was still there, worn with use, but his uncle was not. It made him wonder how long it would take for this house to feel his.

"Supper has been prepared," Mr. Simmons said. "It is ready to serve whenever you are ready."

"Thank you," Caius said.

For once, he'd left Jones behind, feeling like the man probably needed some time to see to his own affairs now he was back in England. It wouldn't be something Jones would initiate, so Caius had done so on his behalf. Or the man had installed himself in some gin palace somewhere and wouldn't leave again until he hadn't a penny left, which was also a distinct possibility. When it came to drinking, it was all or nothing with Jones.

Speaking of drinking. "I think I'll have a whiskey first. What have you got?"

"We have a nice blend from the Glenbrook region."

"Yes, that will do. I think I'll take it in here." Mr. Simmons disappeared and Caius walked to the window. Being early autumn, the evenings were still light. The lawns stretched before him, shaded with the late hour and gray weather. It certainly was peaceful.

It had been a long time since he'd been in such silence. Hong Kong was anything but quiet. The most bustling harbor there was. And London was never peaceful. And quite honestly, the peace and quiet didn't suit his state of mind at the moment, because it immediately returned him to his own behavior yesterday. It bothered him that Eliza thought him a blithering idiot, although he shouldn't care a whit what she thought.

In no uncertain terms had she told him to stay away and cease any direct correspondence with her. Truthfully, he couldn't blame her. Although he wished to communicate his apology and somehow assure her that he didn't act irrationally as a habit. But it was also not a sentiment he wished to convey through solicitors. Apologies were painful enough without having solicitors passing judgment.

No, maybe he should do so in person. Assure her that she hadn't anything to fear from him. Again he cursed his own behavior.

"Here you are, my lord," Mr. Simmons said, carrying a generous glass on a silver tray.

"Thank you," he said, taking the glass and sitting down in his uncle's chair. His uncle had never married. Even with all the pressure to secure an heir, his uncle had instead chosen his brother's child as his heir. In all honesty, there was much about his uncle's life he didn't understand. His leanings had not been toward women. If his uncle's heart had ever belonged to anyone, he didn't know.

Eliza returned to his mind. Why had he been so angry when he'd thought that girl was her child? Deception was one part of it, but there was more to the betrayal than deception. There was also rejection in it. By its very nature, she'd chosen something other than what he offered. Something about him had been inadequate to her. Perhaps it was that even with a child, their child, she had chosen to exclude him.

But none of those assumptions were true. Or rather, the actuality of those assumptions were untrue. Perhaps she would have chosen to exclude him if she had birthed their child.

A small creak signified Mr. Simmons' return and Caius remembered the untouched whiskey in his hand. He wasn't doing a good job progressing the evening for the servants. Taking the glass to his mouth, he swallowed a good portion of it.

It was nice, the slow burn building, the warmth. "I am ready," he said and rose to take himself to the dining room, where Mr. Simmons fussed. It had likely been some months since they'd had anyone to fuss over.

Roast lamb was the main course and it was succulent. Easily the best meal he'd had in a very long time. Compliments were made and the meal thoroughly consumed, and before long, he was back in the library with a second glass of whiskey. He wouldn't have any more tonight, his body had been abused sufficiently the previous night.

The fire crackled as he sat, the cool of night seeping into the house. The servants all retreated to their rooms, and Mr. Simmons was dismissed, the house was silent and still. The distant ticking of a clock was the only thing heard.

When he returned to London, he needed to apologize to Eliza. And he needed to do so in person. Going to her house might be a bit too much of an imposition, but he could do so at her business. Then he could settle this mess he'd created and be done with it. An apology was due. And the days away here would likely settle any ire she had as a consequence and she would be more accepting of his regret.

The decision made, he felt better. Tiredness from the previous late night was starting to wear on him and he yawned. A few more sips of the rather nice whiskey and he would retire, probably wake with the birds in the morning. There was much to do.

Chapter 15:

THERE WAS NO SIGHT of Caius, which was a relief, nor any communication, so Eliza went on with her business as she normally would, currently planning an introductory round for Teresa with all their clients. It was important to inform them all that changes were happening in the business and Teresa was taking over. Teresa's husband might be a complete brute, but at least she was a married woman.

The patrons of charities were often people who wanted to be seen as spotless, and the tarnish of divorce would be more unacceptable with them than most. Some were there for the good they could do, but many were there to bolster their own position in society. It made it both tricky and easier to deal with them, because education for the children of the poor was a concept they liked to support.

"I think it would be good to visit the Colchester Presbytery as well," she said.

"I will be away for quite a few weeks," Teresa said and Eliza could see the concern on her face.

"They will be well," Eliza assured them. Teresa knew this, so it wasn't her children's welfare she worried about as much as how she would miss them. "I wouldn't ask if this wasn't necessary."

"I know," Teresa said brightly, "and I want to."

A sneeze was building up in Eliza's nose and she moved away from the table to violently sneeze. "Bless you," Teresa said.

"Thank you." Another sneeze followed.

"You're not getting ill, are you?"

"No, of course not," she said with a smile and returned to the planning.

But over the next few hours, she started feeling worse. Aches and pains.

"No, I am sure you have a fever coming on," Teresa said, placing her cool hand on Eliza's head. It felt inordinately nice. "You must go home. I will sort the rest of the planning and we'll discuss it after I've finished and you've had a proper rest. No use exerting yourself. Go home. Mr. Henry?" she called loudly.

"What?" he called from somewhere in the warehouse.

"We need a hack."

The yelling was piercing into Eliza's head. It seemed she really was sick and it was trying sitting there. Her whole body ached.

"Now is not the time to exert yourself," Teresa continued. "Off you go. Do you need me to see you home?"

"No, of course not." Eliza wanted to say she was fine enough to walk, but she might not be. Like this, she could run out of energy halfway home, so it was worth investing in a hack. "Fine. I will go," she conceded and sneezed again.

Truthfully, she was feeling a little shaky as she dragged herself up into the hack and the rough movement jarred her senses all the way home, where Mrs. Fisher opened the door for her and fussed.

Before long, she was in bed with a warm towel on her head and copious amounts of blankets.

"We'll have you right as rain in no time," the woman said brightly, but Eliza was distracted by how bright it was.

"Could we close the curtains?"

"Of course," Mrs. Fisher said and walked over to the window, drawing the curtains closed. "Now you sleep. Best thing for it." With that, she left, closing the door to the bedroom behind her. The dark and silence were soothing, but she felt truly horrible.

At points, she woke when Mrs. Fisher entered the room and forced her to drink tea. It tasted strange, so she had no idea what kind of tea the woman was infusing her with.

Horrid dreams followed her, where people chased her and she was surrounded by a general feeling of unpleasantness. She also dreamt of a court of justice, where men were accusing her of being a horrible woman and a sheer failure as a wife. No man should be saddled with such a disgrace, one of them accused. And all throughout, she couldn't open her mouth and speak. She wanted to.

The accusations ringing in her ears, she woke with a start, having no idea where she was. The blankets were wet and clammy, saturated with sweat.

"There you are," Mrs. Fisher said. "And I think your fever may have broken."

"Water," she croaked, her throat feeling impossibly sore. The liquid held to her lips was wonderful, but it did nothing to soothe her throat.

Teresa arrived at the door. "How are you feeling?"

"So terribly I cannot even differentiate between the forms of badness."

"She's much better," Mrs. Fisher filled in and Eliza rolled over, not sure how Mrs. Fisher could say that. "She'll sleep some more, then she'll be right as rain."

"Mmmm," she mumbled, but her throat was agony just with that.

Her room was empty when she woke again, but there was entirely different light. The late afternoon sun, she would guess. She must have slept all night, then all day again. And her nose was entirely blocked.

Weakly, she sat up. No doubt, she was a frightening sight. Blocked nose, fever flushed. Actually, she didn't have the cold or hot sensations fever brought. It must have broken. Her body still felt clammy and she had that distinct unclean feeling. Picking up a lock of hair, she saw her hair was stringy. It only compounded the sense of unease. No doubt if her nose wasn't so blocked, her own odor would be offensive to her.

Rising out of bed, she walked weakly over to her dressing table and poured water into the washing basin. Taking her nightgown off and washing herself. It would make her feel so much better to wash away the fever sweats.

In the mirror, her face was pale and she had blush spots under her eyes. But she no longer had aches and chills, just a pervasive weakness. Still, she washed herself and her hair and she did indeed feel better.

"Ah, you're up," Mrs. Fisher said, carrying a tray of broth. "This will give you some strength."

Without looking, Eliza knew it was bone broth, which she wasn't particularly fond of, but who could argue with centuries of nurses on the healing properties of bones. And truthfully, she couldn't taste a thing. The warmth was somewhat soothing on her throat.

"After," Mrs. Fisher said, "you can have some tea and honey."

The house was quiet. "Everyone is out."

"Yes," Mrs. Fisher answered. "Teresa took the children to stay with a friend."

"Good." Children were always more susceptible to fevers, and Eliza was glad they had been removed from the danger she posed. "I think I have influenza."

"Yes, it appears that way," Mrs. Fisher said, drawing her hands down over her apron as she looked around the room. "And best we wash those sheets."

The woman went about her business as Eliza continued drinking her broth. She felt slightly lightheaded, but it was clear that any danger had passed. She was on the mend—it was just not a nice-looking mend.

"You'll need a supply of handkerchiefs."

"Yes, thank you, Mrs. Fisher. I don't know what I would do without you."

The woman flushed and fussed. "Now you sit and regain your strength." She bundled up the bedsheets and left.

Already, Eliza was bored, having nothing to do. Her mind was too spent to read, but she couldn't sleep anymore. So she dressed in her most loose-fitting morning dress. In fact, she wanted more than broth. Perhaps an egg and some toast.

"What are you doing down here, you silly girl?" Mrs. Fisher chided.

"I can't sit in my room all day. And I thought I might tackle an egg."

"It's a good sign if you're hungry." That seemed to appease the woman. "And I'll bring you some tea with honey. Soothes, it does."

With a nod, Eliza walked into the small parlor and sat down on the worn sofa. They had bought it at the market. It would have been a fine piece once, but now it was old and worn, but still appreciated.

Leaning against the back, she just sat there, waiting to feel better. There wasn't much else to do. She had no idea what Teresa had done with the plans for the charity visits and she probably wouldn't tell if asked.

Her tea arrived and she drank it, and then her egg, which she ate. So no longer hungry, she sat with a blanket on her knees, getting increasingly bored.

A knock sounded at the door, responded to by Mrs. Fisher's purposeful steps. Eliza was curious who could possibly be calling, but perhaps people called here quite often during the day.

"Ah," a man said. "I have come to inquire." The voice was familiar. "I understand Mrs. Hennington has fallen ill." It was Lord Fortescue. Someone must have told him. Why would they, unless he'd called in. "How is she?"

"Mending, but she cannot receive visitors."

"It's alright, Mrs. Fisher," she found herself saying. Perhaps she shouldn't, but she wanted to thank him for his concern.

He appeared in the doorway of the parlor, and he made the space look small.

"Perhaps best not to approach," she said with a smile. "I am flattered with your concern." Maybe she shouldn't have allowed him to see her, considering she was so far below her best. "As you see, I am on the mend."

"I am glad to hear it. I called in at the warehouse and they informed me you had collapsed."

"Overdramatized, I assure you. A touch of fever, but it has passed."

He sat in the chair by the fire, which was only five feet away. If he was shocked by her modest abode, he didn't say so. "I am relieved to hear it. I was concerned you may not have had anyone to care for you."

"Oh, no I assure you, Mrs. Fisher nurses with military precision. But I thank you for your concern."

Her comment made him smile. "Good. Precision is always good in nurses." And she was touched he had worried for her. Although she wasn't entirely sure why he would. Perhaps he was a man who responded when he felt worried abandoned women might be floundering. In her time knowing him, she'd found him cool and aloof, but it was interesting to see that he came to inquire when he worried she might actually be in need. She wasn't sure how to receive such understanding. There might actually be a heart in the man who professed not to have one.

Chapter 16:

CAIUS DIDN'T GET NERVOUS, but if he were to get nervous, it would probably feel like the ill ease he felt right then, sitting in the crested Wickerley carriage outside her warehouse. Apologies were not something he was used to doing, but it was necessary in this case. Well, best to just get on with it.

"This won't take long," he said to the driver as he got out and walked to the entrance where he'd seen her emerge from some days back. He knocked and it took a while for an older man to answer the door. "I need to speak to Mrs. Hennington," he announced.

"She's not here," the man said dismissively, looking him up and down as if he were a sideshow attraction.

"When will she be?"

"I don't know. She's ill."

"Ill?" Caius said with surprise as he'd never known her to be ill. "What sort of illness?"

"They don't share such details with me."

"They?"

"Them, the two of them. Come back some other time," the man said and shut the door. Well, clearly her staff had few manners.

"Ill?" he repeated to a closed door. That hadn't been at all what he'd expected. And who exactly was he referring to with the two of them. Irrational anger simmered again, but he shut it down. Once the anger was dealt with, there was concern. Eliza didn't have the strongest constitution. She was slight and tender. Or at least that had been his perception of her, before he'd learned there were things in her personality he'd never seen. Still, if she was ill, that could be very serious.

"Cavendish Road," he said to the driver as he returned to the carriage. It hadn't been his intention of going to her house, but it hadn't been his intention for her not to be well either.

It didn't take long to get there and he saw the right door and knocked. Again it took some moments before someone answered, and for some reason he'd expected Eliza, not a housekeeper. Couldn't be doing so badly if she had a housekeeper.

"Is Mrs. Hennington here?" he asked.

"Well, I guess you'd better come in too as she is well enough to receive visitors," the woman said tartly. "Mind you, I will only let you stay five minutes."

She indicated to the parlor and he walked in. Eliza's surprise couldn't have been more visible. She looked lost for words and he bowed sharply, before noticing there was another man sitting in a chair by the fire. The room was tiny, so it felt particularly small with three people in it.

Who was this man? Not some laborer by the look of him. A lover, his mind asked. Complete awkwardness descended, and it urged him to speak. "I sought you at your business premises, but they said you were ill. I came to inquire about your health."

"That is very kind of you," Eliza said with an uncertain smile. Granted, she probably wished to entertain two gentlemen in her parlor as much as Caius was happy to be the second gentlemen in her parlor. "I am mending."

Her voice wasn't right and she looked sickly.

"Aah," she started as if she didn't know what to say. "This is Lord Fortescue. Lord Warwick," she said making the introductions. Caius turned to the man and nodded, giving him a moment to assess the man, but he couldn't simply ask who he was and why he was there. Although technically he could.

"Her husband," he filled in.

Understanding seemed to dawn on the man's features, but it didn't make him rise and rush out of there like some bounder being caught in his activities.

"Lord Fortescue is my landlord," Eliza filled in. "In that he owns the warehouse I lease."

"It seems it is not only my instincts that cause me to rush over when I hear you were ill," the man said.

Irrationally, Caius wanted to smash his face in.

"No rush necessary. It is simply a cold. It will pass."

Her nose was congested.

Caius took the only other chair in the small room that had yellow paper on the walls and a palm tree in the corner. The furniture was completely mismatched, but it had a comfortable quality, he had to concede. Not to the standard she'd come from, or even grown up in.

More importantly, why did Eliza and this man have the kind of relationship that he called when she was sick? It required some degree of concern to visit someone who was sick. A degree of concern well beyond a landlord, but that was how she'd introduced him.

The way he sat did not suggest he was comfortable in this house. And by the look of him, he was a man who could keep his mistresses in better accommodation than this. Caius could only assume the man wanted her as his mistress. Why else would he be here?

"I'd offer tea to you gentlemen," the harridan housekeeper said from the door, "but you both have to leave in a minute."

"Thank you, Mrs. Fisher," Eliza said reassuringly.

A quiet awkwardness descended again. As for his apology, it wasn't something he could deliver in front of an audience, particularly in front of a man who Caius suspected had some intention and hope.

Chapter 17:

WITH A SIGH, ELIZA sat and stared out the window. At times, she wished for time with nothing to do, but now that she was sitting at home with nothing to do, it was exceedingly dull. The house was quiet with the children gone, and Eliza had no idea what was happening with the planning or the production delivery that was scheduled to arrive.

Her throat was hoarse, but she felt much better. Rising again, she paced around the small room, wondering if she should go for a walk and get some fresh air, but Mrs. Fisher would balk at the idea, claiming she would weaken somewhere along the way and that disaster would ensue.

Also, she could reflect on the dreadfully awkward meeting of Lord Fortescue and Caius. It seemed neither of them was particularly pleased to see the other and it had just been tense and uncomfortable. Obviously, Eliza blamed Caius, because awkward and uncomfortable seemed to be his purview. And she couldn't understand why he'd arrived at all, especially after she'd explicitly told him not to communicate directly with her.

Accusations had not flown and finding a man in her parlor would probably give his theories of her utter inadequacy some credence, but he hadn't uttered a word. In a way, she felt it served him right for dropping in unannounced. Maybe she'd confirmed the worst of his expectations. Most likely, he believed them to be lovers cuckolding him. But why had he not vented his disgust? It wasn't as if Caius feared another man's reaction. That was not how he thought.

A knock on the door made her pause, but she realized it was around the time the mailman came, so it probably wasn't visitors descending on her.

As she sat down again, she heard Mrs. Fisher head for the door and then hushed voices spoke and the door closed again.

"A letter, Mrs. Hennington," she said, appearing at the door with a letter in hand. With a smile, Eliza accepted it, seeing Caius' watermark on the back of the envelope. Again he wasn't communicating through solicitors as she'd requested.

Tapping the envelope on her fingers, she wondered if she wanted to open it, almost fearing it would make her angry. Being sick, she could justify avoiding anything aggravating, but she was also too curious. Would this be fresh accusations aimed at her, that she was cavorting with men perhaps?

With a groan, she opened the letter and unfolded the stiff parchment. It was his handwriting. It'd been a long time since she'd seen it, or since he'd written her a letter. There had been a time when receiving a letter from him had been the most exciting thing in the entire world. A flash of sadness washed through her for a moment, but she pushed it away to focus on what renewed unpleasantness was about to accost.

But it wasn't unpleasantness. Instead it was an apology for his behavior, which he admitted was utterly irrational. Words he used in his letter. It specifically referred to the day outside her warehouse. Not the preceding years and the misery related to that. That was all the letter said, that he apologized for his behavior and that he couldn't account for it.

Putting it to side for a moment, she stared at it, not quite sure what it meant. Was he genuinely sorry for how he'd behaved, or was this a response to her forbidding him from communicating with her directly?

A groan escaped her as she leaned her cheeks into her hands. When she'd wished for something to do, it hadn't been to deal with Caius.

Another knock sounded at the door. It couldn't be the mailman this time and Eliza straightened as she feared Caius was following up his apology with an in-person visit. Surely not. What did he want?

A man's voice was heard at the door when Mrs. Fisher went to answer, but she didn't immediately recognize Caius' voice. Perhaps she didn't anymore.

"Lord Fortescue is here to see you," Mrs. Fisher announced.

"Please see him in," she replied and hid Caius' letter within a stack of books. She was both curious and worried about why Lord Fortescue wanted to see her again. Had seeing Caius made him less open to her continuing with the lease? Men sometimes had odd loyalties to each other, and some men felt they wouldn't wish to trespass within another man's marriage. Even if that marriage was ending.

Again she noted how he seemed to fill the room and a flush spread across her cheeks as he took her hand and kissed it. "You seem better," he said. "I brought you these." A bag of oranges was handed over to her.

"Oh, thank you. I love oranges."

"My mother has an orangery. She says they are superb for fighting colds."

"They are orbs of happiness in any case," Eliza said with a smile. Oranges were indeed a very considerable gift. "I will enjoy them immensely."

Lord Fortescue took a seat and there was a moment of awkwardness as if neither of them knew what to say, and truthfully, she didn't know the reason for this visit, but hoped it was simply to call on her. Was it so bad to hope for?

On some level, she feared men's interest in her, worried that their intentions were less than honorable. With him, however, she'd had enough dealings with to hope he didn't have the perception of her that she was willing to be a man's mistress.

How she would feel post the divorce, she wasn't sure, particularly with an unmarried man such as Lord Fortescue. A married man, she would never have any interest or intentions with. But would she be willing to carry on an acquaintance with a man who could not see himself marrying a divorcée? In all honesty, she wasn't sure she wanted to marry again, but the question of if she would swear off all men for the rest of her life remained to be answered.

In all the years she'd been separated from her husband, she refused to even entertain the idea, preferring to be loyal to her vows, even if he'd utterly rejected her. Saying that, she was about to be divorced, which released her from her vows and any obligation she held herself to. And she wasn't a young miss anymore, but a woman who'd been married—even if in reality that marriage itself had been inordinately short.

The future was for her to determine. It was a liberating and exciting feeling after all the heartache and misery. That time was coming to an end and she needed to build a new life for herself. In many ways, she had with her business, but there was also a personal life to consider. And she wondered if Lord Fortescue wished to be a part of that.

"I am glad to see you are better," he said.

"Yes, every day I seem a little stronger."

It looked as though there was something he wished to say, but he couldn't find the words for it. "I have enjoyed making your acquaintance," he started and Eliza felt her tension harden as this sounded like some kind of determination on their ongoing relationship. "And I understand you are facing some rough weather, through which I hope to be a steady friend."

Eliza considered her words. "A friendship I am grateful for, because many would not extend friendship to women in my position."

"Then they are foolish and judgmental. We shouldn't be judged for relationships that fundamentally don't suit us."

For a while, it had seemed that her relationship with Caius suited her perfectly, but it had fallen apart completely and utterly. In that sense, it didn't suit at all, did it?

"I suppose what I wish to say is that I do not judge you for a failed marriage. I have learned that some things that appear perfect on the surface are anything but. Things are never so simple."

"No, I suppose not," she said, her opinion of him growing because he seemed capable of seeing beyond the immediate. Also because he was secure enough as a person to not waver at the face of judgment from others who didn't see beyond the immediate. Because there were people who felt she was better off dead rather than as a divorced woman. It was encouraging to see there were people who didn't dismiss her entirely because of this thing that was to happen to her. Many were happy to assign the fault to her and to have her suffer no comeback as a result.

"I find all storms eventually pass," he said. "As will this one."

"I must admit, I look forward to that point, when everything is… sorted."

"Well, you can depend on my assistance if you should require it. During or after. It is important not to stop taking time for one's own benefit. So in that light, I would like to invite you to the theatre one evening."

"Oh," Eliza said, feeling her cheeks color. "That is very… interesting." Was that a silly term? She couldn't think of another. "I would perhaps…" Should she wait for such things for after the divorce was concluded? Yes, probably. She could imagine it being reported that she was cavorting with other men if people saw her at the theatre. "Yes, that would be very enjoyable, but I suspect more so when there isn't quite so much attention stirred."

Not only in terms of attention, but for her, there was a demarcation between being a married woman and not, and that would happen with the judge's gavel.

If he wished to take her out to the theatre after, there was no reason she shouldn't go.

"Then I will look forward to it. In the meantime, you can depend on my friendship."

Relief showed on his face, as if communicating his sentiments had been a burden weighing on him, and now it seemed they had reached an understanding. It had been a very long time since she'd had an understanding of this kind with a man—the kind of understanding that suggested he liked her and that they should spend some time in each other's company. There was something inherently exciting about it, about the prospects contained in such an understanding.

Chapter 18:

IN SOME RESPECTS, Caius knew he had no right to be upset about finding Lord Fortescue in Eliza's house. But equally, they hadn't even started the divorce process yet and men were sniffing around her already. For all he knew, men could have been sniffing around her for years, done far worse than sniffing too. In fact, all likelihood pointed in that direction judging by how their marriage had effectively ended. His focus now would be on the complete ending of the marriage. And not to be distracted by what Eliza did with herself.

It only went to show that this was all necessary, didn't it? He'd known that for a while, and if she debased herself with men, it was for her conscience to bear. If she had any decency, she would carry out her affairs with discretion.

As for Fortescue, the man wasn't someone Caius was familiar with, and he'd forbid himself to enquire about the man. He wasn't important. If not him, it would probably be some other man. Eliza seemed to have some irrational need to draw the attention of men. It was the only thing that could explain her behavior during their marriage.

No, this only provided more proof of her adulterous nature. If he asked around, there was probably a string of men she'd cavorted with in the time he'd been away. Granted she'd been discreet until now, or Octavia would have regaled him with the tales. Hopefully that discretion would continue, but there would be closer scrutiny of her activities during the divorce.

"The mail arrived," Jones said, placing a pile of letters on his desk.

"Right," Caius said and reached for them. The typical type of communications. Invitation to social engagements, also parties seeking to explore investment opportunities.

Then there was a letter unlike the others. Turning it over, he saw it was from Mrs. Moore. Largely he'd forgotten he'd sent queries to her and about William Castle Garrick, as with Eliza's agreement to plead guilty, the need to track the man wasn't as important. Unfortunately, Eliza's agreement to do so had come after he'd sent the letter to the woman.

At the least, he needed to write the woman to say his original request was unnecessary and he was sorry to waste her time.

Grabbing the brass penknife from the desk, he slid it in and cut the envelope open. The letter itself was on thin paper that crinkled when he opened it. He read the short missive which said she was happy to answer any questions he had about that 'bounder' if he called. Interesting that she referred to him as a bounder.

It went on to say Castle Garrick was an interesting character and that he should take care if he has any dealings with the man.

Caius had to admit he found the letter intriguing. Again, it wasn't necessary to follow up on this anymore, but this woman's scathing view on William Castle Garrick was curious. The man had been his friend for quite some time, until the awkwardness of it all had ruined the friendship.

Still, this woman had a poor opinion of the man, and there was a good chance it had nothing to do with his activities in England.

Perhaps he should go and see her. It would be prudent in case something should arise that would call this man's reputation into question. Not that it could have much of an impact if Eliza was pleading guilty. And it would be rude to not see the lady who'd so kindly availed her time. He would go in the morning, he decided.

So that left this evening to deal with, and he was in too foul a mood to enjoy himself, so a social engagement was out of the question—more so as he hadn't responded to any. And a night out in some gaming hell would probably lead to a drunken fight the mood he was in. No, he didn't want to deal with people. Neither did he want to sit there and muse on the things Eliza would find attractive about that ridiculous man.

Surprisingly, there was little to do in London when in a foul mood. So he moved to the fire and sat there with a glass of whiskey that he wasn't particularly enjoying, to wile away some hours before he could go to bed.

*

The weather held nicely the next day, so he rode to Mrs. Moore's house in Highgate. In no particular hurry, perhaps because now that he was about to hear about William Castle Garrick's high jinx, he wasn't all that enthusiastic about it. Perhaps because it would bring back feelings and emotions from the past, and he wasn't particularly keen on suffering from either feelings or emotions. Concepts that had never served him well.

Highgate was a lovely town. Slow and sedate, filled with cottages and flowers. Most importantly, it lacked the chaos of London's streets.

With the help of a messenger boy, he found Mrs. Moore's house without much trouble and a nearby stable boy offered to care for his horse.

Mrs. Moore seemed like a lovely lady, although her house smelled like boiled cabbage. It wasn't large, but comfortable for an elderly woman.

She smiled as he sat down. "I am pleased to make your acquaintance. It is always fun when visitors come, particularly ones I haven't met before."

Her blue eyes were surveying him intently, and Caius knew this was a woman who paid attention. "Well, it was a lovely ride over."

"Autumn is a lovely season. One does miss it when having to live without it. The tropics are very one-directional in terms of the weather. It rains or it doesn't. Much more nuanced here, rains, showers, drizzle. They're all very distinct."

"Yes, I suppose you're right," Caius said, making himself comfortable in his seat and hoping this wasn't going to be the kind of visit where this woman divulged the entire contents of her head.

"Now, William Castle Garrick. Friend of yours, is he?"

"Well. I thought so. We were at Oxford together."

"Oh, I see. So he didn't lie about that."

Caius' head twisted to the side with the statement. Clearly this woman thought him a liar. "There was an incident and we parted company."

"I am sorry to hear that, but I cannot say I'm surprised. If you don't mind me asking, I am curious to know the nature of the incident."

"It relates to my wife."

"Ah," the woman said. "In truth, I think the man is a misogynist."

Caius' eyebrows rose. The man must have changed, because from what Caius had seen of William, he charmed women inordinately.

"Was there an accusation?" she asked intently and her eyebrows now drew together. Caius stilled, feeling concerned where this was going. Had the man been bragging about his conquests?

"Yes."

She chuckled. "It seems to be what he does."

"I don't understand."

"Well, in Jamaica, he accused one of the daughters of the Governor of impropriety, but he was careless and was found out."

"Careless how? What do you mean?" Caius said a little more forcefully.

"It seemed he didn't put much planning into his campaign to destroy this girl's character and he chose a night of this supposed impropriety where she was attended by no less than her parents, the doctor and the village priest. It couldn't have happened as he'd claimed at all. With such a grave mistake, he had to flee quick-smart, or the Governor himself would have had the man up on charges. So if you were hoping to find him, I can tell you that he will not be coming back to Jamaica anytime soon."

"I don't understand," Caius repeated, even as that wasn't true. The implications of what the man had done were sinking in, and it was the most awful feeling Caius could imagine. About as awful as being told his lovely wife had been deceptive. "Why would he do such a thing?"

"It turns out he seeks to destroy women, particularly those who spurn him."

The room was unbearably hot for a moment.

"As I said, quite the misogynist. So I'm not surprised to learn he has made such accusations before. If one were to look, I am sure he's done so more than once. I'm sure a man like that cares nothing about the consequences of his accusations, he seeks the consequences."

"Why would a man do that?"

"Why would a man destroy a woman?" she asked as if it was a stupid question. "Because he hates women."

"No, I knew the fellow. He wasn't like that."

She was silent for a moment as if considering. "Perhaps he wasn't. Or perhaps he didn't divulge his hatred. Men can show very different sides of themselves to women, sides they hide otherwise."

Furtively, Caius tried to think back to their time at Oxford. Yes, there had always been lewd jokes, and William had always been the one that hassled the barmaids. There had been dismissal there, but to Caius' shame, he admitted it wasn't all that unusual, so they had never paid it much attention. Young men were dismissive of girls, but it didn't mean they would purposefully destroy a marriage.

Because it had destroyed his life as well. "No, I cannot account for it," Caius admitted. "Why would a friend do that?"

"It is hard to account for how such a man's mind works. I suppose his opinion of women is so poor, he didn't perceive the loss of a marriage. Or his hatred of being spurned is so strong, he doesn't care as long as he harms the one spurning him. Not all think through the consequences of what they do."

That was true. In the military, those men could be incredibly destructive and had to be placed where they could do little harm.

Was it true that he was actually the victim of such a man? That his marriage was felled by a hateful act?

Looking back at his memories now, there was consistency in the dismissal William Castle Garrick showed towards women, lewd talk and small acts of viciousness. His mind ran over the things he remembered, and had dismissed as drunken loutishness. But viewed as a whole, there was consistency there.

Heat pumped through his body and he really wanted to hit something, in particularly the bounder who was the cause of all this. His marriage was destroyed by this man's accusations, and he hadn't cared if the accusations were true or not. In fact, it could be that this man's accusations only came when they weren't true. Rejection drove them.

The need to move coursed through his body, but he was currently sitting in an elderly woman's parlor and had to restrain himself.

"This is..." he started. "Thank you for your time. I appreciate it." When nothing else worked, falling back on ingrained politeness was the best course of action. "I must go," he said, rising sharply.

"I am sorry to hear that you may have been a victim of this man," she said, but Caius was only half listening. Anger pierced him and he needed to get out of there.

"My best regards for your future and happiness." He was babbling what sounded like an adequate goodbye and found his way out of the house into fresh air. With firm strides, he walked past the confused stable boy and down the street, having no idea where he was going.

His marriage ended due to a false accusation. That bastard had come in and destroyed everything and then left a mess behind him. Years of misery. Years spent in the Far East to get away from the mess.

If William were to appear right then, Caius would probably run him through with a sword, except he didn't have a sword. Probably he would settle for beating the man to death. And he wasn't a man to lose his temper, but right now... This was too much to dismiss.

Chapter 19:

CAIUS ARRIVED AT Denham Hall after dark. It had been a couple of days of riding, and he hadn't intended on riding all the way there, but after his meeting with Mrs. Moore and the shocking revelations uncovered, he'd needed time to think.

A complete hash. That was the only conclusion for it, and as he was riding, there hadn't been the time to think like he'd wanted, but distraction, because this wasn't something he could defeat with logic. A despicable lie had messed up his entire life and now he had to sit with the fact that Eliza might be innocent of the charges laid against her. In all likelihood she was innocent.

Being on horseback, no one saw him coming, so he had to knock on the door to be let in. It was his sister that answered, looking searchingly out into the darkness. "Caius? What are you doing here? Is everything alright?"

"Yes, fine," he lied. Well, no one was dead, which was what she was really asking. But, no, everything was not fine.

"We weren't expecting you. Did you send a letter? It must have gone astray."

"It's more of an impulsive visit."

"Come in. Father's in the parlor. As is Julius. They'll be pleased to see you. We're discussing the plans for the harvest celebrations."

Rural things like harvest celebrations weren't on his mind much these days. "Right," he said as he followed his sister into the warm parlor. So many evenings he'd sat there as a young man. A few of those with Eliza as his bride. Renewed unease swept through him, as it had periodically since he left Mrs. Moore's house.

"Caius," his father said. "This is a surprise. Have you been to Bickerley yet?"

"Yes, I have gone," he said as he sat down and nodded yes when Mr. Phillips enquired if he wanted a glass of whiskey. It was too late to join them for supper. And the way his stomach felt, he wasn't sure he could manage a meal. "Everything is fine there. The staff are competent and it is well managed."

"That's lucky," Octavia said. "It would be horrible to have to come in and dismiss people from their positions."

"Well, it seems the only one truly incompetent is me," Caius admitted. The time had passed when he feared admitting shortcomings to his father. A feeble person hid things and this was a big thing—too big to hide.

"And with which skill do you rate yourself incompetent?" Julius asked, echoing the competitiveness from their past.

"Marriage, it seems."

"Yes well, you chose very poorly," his father said.

"As it happens, perhaps I didn't. Recent revelations suggest that Eliza may indeed have been… innocent."

"Well, she would say that," Octavia said dismissively.

"Oddly, she hasn't, but I have it from good authority that William Castle Garrick has a habit of falsely accusing women of adultery."

"No, why would he do such a thing?" Octavia said, now concerned. "That's preposterous. You have no cause to doubt yourself."

"It seems he has been caught doing it to a rather prominent daughter in the West Indies, and was driven from the area as a liar and a bounder."

Silence descended on the room.

"Are you sure?" Julius asked, his eyebrows drawn tight.

"How am I to know? I wasn't there in the room, but there is firm evidence that he has a tendency to lie about such things."

"Well, what does Eliza say?"

"We have not discussed it, but she has said she will plead guilty to adultery at the trial."

"There you go then. Straight from the horse's mouth. She accepts her guilt."

It was a guilty plea she exchanged for her business, an act of someone who was cutting their losses. If he was in her position, he would probably do exactly the same. "At the time, she always professed her innocence, didn't she?"

"It was so long ago, we cannot recall exactly what she said," Julius pointed out.

The truth was that he hadn't listened to her at the time as he had taken the accusation as fact. Nothing she'd said had made a bit of difference. He'd dismissed everything coming out of her mouth. But he did recall there had been a moment where she'd stopped talking. At the time he'd taken it as relief that she had finally acknowledged that she couldn't talk her way out of it. But in fact, perhaps she had simply given up.

Internally he winced. "A gargantuan cockup," he finally said.

No one said anything further.

"If that is the case," his father finally said, "and she is pleading guilty, it sounds as if the lady wants to be shot of you."

"You did abandon her for six years," Octavia said, remarkably quick at shifting the blame where a moment before, she'd been so assured in Eliza's guilt, she'd even defended William Castle Garrick against the accusations laid against him.

"I supported her," Caius stated. "She had a stipend throughout the time I was gone."

"She may have made plans in your absence. For all we know, she has an entirely different life now."

The annoying Lord Fortescue came to mind. Clearly a man who had bad intentions. Eliza should know better than to have men call at her house. Then again, she would be an unmarried woman sometime in the near future. And men were obviously sniffing around her.

This time, his groan wasn't entirely internal. Eliza had a business, and a life that did not include him. A life that actively sought his absence, it would seem. Her willingness to plead guilty only proved that she wished to cut herself from this marriage as quickly and painlessly as she could.

His mind hurt from thinking about it all. There had been too much thinking since the moment he'd left Mrs. Moore. Never had a visit to a kindly old gossip left him so disturbed and undone. "I think I will retire. I am exhausted," he admitted. Both physically and spiritually, he was exhausted.

Leaving his family behind, he took his glass of whiskey with him, back to the room he'd shared with her throughout their short marriage. All signs of her had been removed. Something he'd dictated after he'd put her in a carriage and had sent her packing.

And all along, she'd been innocent of the accusations against her. It had ended her marriage and had left her without a home. Another thing he'd been too angry to consider at the time. He'd felt it had served her right.

Truthfully, he would quite happily strangle William Castle Garrick right now if he could get his hands around the man's neck. Just the degree of heartache and misery the man had caused. It was still unfathomable that someone would do that. And to a friend. It was simply inconceivable.

If he'd owed an apology to Eliza for yelling at her in the street for baseless and irrational conclusions, how could he possibly apologize for this?

His father's suggestion to simply ignore this truth he'd learned and continue on this course had some practical merits. It could well be the best for everyone involved. Eliza had a life that did not include him, and it seemed a suitor—provided his intentions were honorable. Surely she had to know how some men would see her now. Her vulnerable state would attract a less than honorable lot, seeking to capitalize on her desperation.

But it wasn't desperation he'd perceived from her. Exasperation perhaps. No, Eliza was made of sterner things. When her life had been ruined, she'd built a business to support herself, and to find meaning in her life. She'd gone on without him, and had done so successfully. Unlikely would she fall for some bounder seeking to use her—especially as she'd already been the victim of a true bounder.

Hopefully she would show some care in her assessment of this Lord Fortescue as well. And for all intents and purposes, it wasn't any of his business who she associated with. Or it wouldn't be very soon.

Lying down on the bed, he groaned and blocked the light from his eyes with the back of his hand. Yes, this was a monumental cockup, probably the biggest in his life. And while it might be better for all to pretend he hadn't learnt what he'd been told by Mrs. Moore. The truth was that he had, and he wasn't a man who hid from the truth, no matter how inconvenient—or how much he wanted to. It was simply not the man he was, and a principle he would not compromise.

Chapter 20:

IT WAS NICE TO BE back at work. Eliza felt good, strong compared to what she had been, but she'd had enough time sitting in her parlor being bored. Although the visits from Lord Fortescue had been much appreciated. And there was an excitement about him that she carried with her—even as she knew she shouldn't place any hopes there. She just couldn't help it.

The very idea of having a beau was exciting, particularly after six long years when she wouldn't even look at a man. But now, the end of her marriage was in sight, as was any obligation she had to her vows.

And the best thing was that Fontescue knew that about her past and wasn't scared away. That said something very important about the man, didn't it?

But it was time for some food and she tended to go across the road to the bakery at midday. They had lovely cheese rolls and occasionally she'd indulge in something sweet. Right now, she was perfectly happy to feel well in her body again. Perhaps even well in her life and prospects—once the divorce was over. As Fortescue said, this storm would pass and there often was calm, pleasant weather after a storm.

"Eliza," she heard as she walked across the road. The hair along her arms rose, because she knew that voice.

Pausing, she turned to see Caius, looking dark and dapper. The years away hadn't tarnished his handsomeness. Oh the lengths she'd thought about his handsomeness as they'd been courting. She hadn't believed her luck that such a man had been interested in her. But like anything that had felt too good to be true, it had fallen apart.

"Caius," she said, quelling the urge to turn on her heels and walk away. "You have come to see me again. That's... considerate. I am quite well if you're inquiring?"

"Excuse me?" he said absently, looking confused. Clearly he wasn't here to see if she'd recovered from her illness. And it seemed this was another thing that couldn't be left to the solicitors to deal with.

"How can I assist you, Caius?"

"Uhmm," he started, not looking her in the eyes, which suggested this conversation was to be awkward and uncomfortable. So how about they don't have it? "Could we have a word?"

"We are having a word, right now. State your business and we can both go."

"It is a little more delicate in nature."

"Nothing we have going on between us is delicate in nature. Please just state what you want and then go."

"You never professed that what William Castle Garrick said was true."

"What?"

"You never admitted what he said was true. You always denied it."

"I told you I would plead guilty and I intend to keep my word. You will have your guilty plea. We have an agreement."

Annoyance dripped like ice along her nerves, and she crossed her arms. Why was he here? What did he want? Was he some kind of masochist who wanted details about this supposed tryst she'd had with that man?

With straight back, he regarded her. There was discomfort in him. "It has come to my attention that William Castle Garrick has made a habit of lying about such things."

Eliza blinked. For so long that was the one thing she'd wanted him to say. She'd wanted him to see what had happened, but he'd refused to. But it was too late now. None of this mattered now. "What that man does is irrelevant. You have your guilty plea. I am very busy and I must go. Good day."

Mostly she had to get away from there because she could feel tears tickling the back of her eyes. Why would he come and say such a thing now? What was the point of it? Was this some means to torture her?

With quick steps, she walked away.

"Because if the accusations he made are untrue, and I think they are, then we have no grounds for divorce," he called.

Eliza's step faltered, but she refused to turn around. She only half turned back. "You have no idea what I have done in the time you have been gone."

"What have you done in the time I was gone?"

The truth was, nothing. She'd done nothing but circumvent her marriage vows and now she was being punished for it. "None of your business," she said sharply. "You ensured that."

Unwilling to listen to another word, Eliza marched away, her steps sharp, covering as much ground as she could. She had no idea where she was going, but tears were threatening, and she made her way into an alley before the sobs came.

How could he do this to her? Why? What was the point of this? They had set the course. It could not change now. And then to come along and say the things she'd wanted him to say, years too late? What was the point of that? It was stupid and it was cruel.

Wracking sobs came and then subsided, and she stood leaning her forehead against the cool bricks of a wall. It stunk in this alley, she realized, but she felt reticent leaving the safety of the alley in case he roamed out there.

Tentatively she stepped out, but he wasn't in sight. Her appetite had completely fled, so she walked back to the warehouse and took herself to her office where she closed the door, hoping to shut the world out.

With heaviness, she sat down in her chair, not sure she now was as recovered as she'd thought. Her energy had fleeted entirely.

Chapter 21:

GRIMLY, CAIUS STARED at the fire, sitting by the chair in near darkness. It had been a tormenting few days, and then the particularly grim task of informing Eliza of what he'd learnt. He could still recall Eliza's shocked dismay, and how she'd rushed to get away from him. Although what he'd expected, he didn't know. Going to see her had been a kneejerk reaction.

"Would you like some candles lit?" Mr. Jones asked.

He shook his head. "The dark suits me at the moment."

"Is everything alright, my lord?"

Caius didn't answer for a while. "Have you ever been falsely accused of something?"

"Can't say that I have. Not so I recall in any case. But I have known men who have been."

"And what should be done in such cases?"

"Things must be put right. Often, I have found, there are vested interests in sweeping such things away."

Caius suspected Mr. Jones was talking of things in the military, where accusations could have severe consequences. Still, there were always those who wished to ignore travesties of justice to save the embarrassment of making the wrong decision.

While there may be no hanging involved here, the consequences for Eliza were severe, and she'd been doing her best to mitigate them.

"Even if the victim also wants things swept under the carpet?"

"It would still be a lie," Mr. Jones stated, and Caius shifted uncomfortably in his seat. Not only was it a lie, but it would be breaking what was in essence sacred vows. In front of God and people in their lives, he stood in front of a priest and promised he would take care of her.

By providing her a stipend, he'd felt he'd discharged his obligations to the same level that she had hers. Except that part hadn't been true. "Yes, a lie," Caius said absently. "Thank you. You can retire. I shall need nothing else tonight."

With a quick nod, Mr. Jones left, leaving Caius feeling no better. No better, but newly determined. To continue with this divorce would be propagating a lie. And any way you cut, it wasn't right. Eliza had never broken her vows.

As she'd pointed out, he had no idea what she'd done in his absence, especially as she was entertaining a man in her parlor when he'd come to call. But then how could he blame her for what she'd done after he'd deserted the marriage, particularly now that divorce was impending.

Except it wasn't, because their grounds for divorce was as big a lie as what William Castle Garrick had claimed. And continuing with this divorce then had to be as gravely wrong.

Getting up, he moved to his desk and pulled a piece of letter parchment toward him and wrote to his solicitors, explaining that the divorce would not proceed. Carefully he folded it and melted wax to seal it.

When done, it sat on his desk and he felt better. However they were to proceed with this, it wasn't going to be through the means of a lie.

And Eliza would not have her reputation decimated in the press and every salon in the country. That would be spared her, but he also knew that she wouldn't be happy with this decision. If she would come to understand it, he didn't know. Her reaction when he'd spoken to her suggested she wouldn't be pleased.

Truthfully, he left lighter than he had in years. With this decision made, his mood changed entirely and it didn't suit now to glumly sit by the fire and commiserate. In fact, he wanted a drink, and he wondered if he should walk over to the pub a few streets over. It wasn't the best pub in town, and its selection of whiskey was mediocre at best, but right now, he wanted a drink, and maybe even people around him while he had it.

*

His head pounded as he woke to bright sunlight in the morning, having forgotten to draw the curtains last night. There had been a few whiskeys, particularly as his newly found drinking mate had mistakenly assumed that he was getting married, when he'd tried to explain that he had decided not to un-marry.

It had been a nice evening, probably the happiest one he'd spent in quite a while. Making a friend like one only did in a drinking establishment. A friendship that would last only one night, but curiously congenial for it.

Whatever he'd felt about not getting divorced, it had a significant consequence in that he and Eliza were still married and would continue to be married, and their relationship was in tatters. There were no grounds for divorce, hence they would not divorce.

The discussion with her the previous day hadn't gone well. It had been a shock to her—he'd seen it on her face. In a way, they'd both suffered shocks in the last few days, so now it was perhaps time to discover what they had and what they could do.

He needed to speak to her again, but it wouldn't be easy doing so. Leaning over, he picked up his watch and saw it was well past nine. Eliza would probably have left the house already. She wouldn't be there for him to simply call on her. In fact, most of their discussions tended to be on the street, except that time when she'd been sick and that man had attended her.

Perhaps one of the things they needed to establish was to what degree that man was in her life. Her landlord, she'd said when she'd introduced them. By the looks of it, he wasn't overly at ease in her house, so it didn't seem as if he'd spent any degree of time there. But there were intentions with a man who visited a sick lady. This man had some intention with Eliza. That much was clear.

It constituted a truly awkward situation, but the fact was that he and Eliza were still married and they were not getting a divorce. They had no cause to. She'd done nothing wrong. And after he'd abandoned her, he could hardly blame her for making a life for herself. Because the truth was that he'd abandoned her. Renewed unease washed through him. Why had he not listened? She'd tried to tell him, but he'd refused to hear it. And then he'd sent her packing. Not just that, but he'd left the country, specifically so he would be out of her reach. So that he didn't have to think or talk about her.

All the wrongs he had done her and then threatened to divorce her.

So this man, who in some way was in her life, perhaps Caius should simply be grateful that the man hadn't harmed her, because her husband had certainly not been there to defend her against anyone who'd sought to.

All in all, he'd been a terrible husband. On some level, it was understandable that she wanted to not veer from the course they were on.

No, it would be best to see her at that warehouse where she seemed to spend most of her days. Perhaps if she was amenable, they could discuss things in a nearby pub or coffee house. But he wasn't sure amenable was her intent at the moment. Truthfully, he wasn't sure how she would take this. Obviously she knew they had no grounds for divorce.

A soft knock sounded at his door and he answered. As expected, Mr. Jones had arrived to deliver a letter.

Tension rose inside him as he wondered if it was from Eliza, but saw his sister's handwriting. Most of the letters he'd received in the last few years had been from his sister, so he knew her handwriting well. Cracking the seal, he opened. She was coming to visit, it seemed. Likely she wanted a front row seat in this debacle, he thought bitterly.

Putting it to side, he forgot about it, having bigger things to worry about today than the forthcoming arrival of his sister. Dressing, he didn't waste time, even if a cup of coffee would do wonders for any lingering effects from the night before.

Having decided what to do, he wanted to get this over with. Easier than to let such things linger on his mind. Only once they'd had this discussion would he know where they stood from her perspective.

It could be that today she saw it as a relief as a divorce would be devastating for her life, including her business. As she dealt with charities, they wouldn't take well to dealing with a divorced woman. Saving this marriage would save the business too.

Many wouldn't like to see their wives engaged with such a business, but it seemed to be a passion for her and he would support her any way he could. That could perhaps be an ice breaker for this conversation they were just about to have.

"I will be going out for a while," he said to Mr. Jones when he returned. "I will ride, I think."

Mr. Jones nodded and went off to tell the stable lad. And Caius waited in his hallway for his horse to be brought to him. He hated to admit it, but he was nervous to face Eliza. At the same time, he was hopeful. This could be a new start for them. They could erase all the unfortunate unpleasantness that had been and start again. It was interesting to think that was possible.

Chapter 22:

ELIZA SIMPLY STARED at Mr. Henry open-mouthed as he stood waiting on her answer for if he could show her husband in. It's not a good time, she wanted to say, but she had also known this was coming, so she chided herself for being a coward. This had to be faced.

"Yes, I suppose," she said with little heart. "And then perhaps leave us to our discussion."

The older man looked at her for a moment. "You sure?"

"Quite sure."

Teresa was on her way to Bournemouth, which meant she could not be depended on to assist if this turned out to be uncomfortable. Not that she expected Caius to be violent in any way, as perhaps Teresa would fear from her own history with husbands.

As she waited, she wrung her hands together. "Caius," she said as he appeared and closed the door. They could still be seen, and from the corner of her eye, she saw Mr. Henry lurking. It was nice that he was concerned, but she should have told him it was entirely unnecessary. Caius was not a violent man, but then again, who knew how he'd changed with the passing years.

He wore dark clothes today, finely tailored and she wondered if his clothes were new and more fitting of Lord

Warwick. As usual, he never failed to be handsome. The age serving his face well.

"Do I take it that by your appearance here, you have concocted a solution to our situation?"

"Yes, I have reached a solution."

Nervousness bit deep inside her stomach, but she wasn't entirely sure why.

"We are to remain married."

"What? No!"

"As I said, we have no cause for divorce."

"If it is cause you need, I am sure I can provide some."

His jaw was tight and he wasn't looking at her. This wasn't something he relished. Neither of them seemed to, just like every time they spoke. He shifted slightly. "I cannot blame you for the things you have done since I abandoned you."

It was the first time he admitted that he'd abandoned her. During the meeting with the solicitors, he'd said the opposite, that by providing her with a monthly stipend, he hadn't abandoned her. Legally, that was the case.

"Well that is very magnanimous that you forgive me for..." her voice faltered and she couldn't finish the sentence. Her anger and outrage threatened to overwhelm her, but she was trying to calm herself.

"And I'm not entirely sure how we will continue. Cordially, I hope. In time perhaps—"

"In time?" She couldn't believe what she was hearing. Did he have some notion that they could simply pick up where they'd left off? No, that was not possible. "No," she said flatly. "As inordinately pleased I am that you forgive me," she said, trying to rein in her sarcasm. "The truth is that I do not forgive you."

"I admit that I bear responsibility."

"You failed utterly. I did nothing wrong and you wouldn't even listen to me. What good were you as a husband? What good are you as a husband? You failed at the very first hurdle. Such a husband is not worth having." Words were coming out of her mouth and she had no control over them. It was the truth, and it flowed straight from her heart and out of her mouth.

"Yes," was all he said. Again he refused to look at her and that only made her more angry.

"So I don't want to be married to you. I want someone better." Again she had no control over what she was saying, but still, she couldn't regret it. "I want to put this behind me and never think about it, or you again."

"But we cannot."

"You say that. You are the one saying we can't."

"Because you didn't break your vows."

"What do vows mean now? What vows did you keep?"

"We do not have grounds for divorce."

"How do you know? You don't know me at all. And I have come to realize that you never did."

"That is not true."

"Really? Because you seemed to not have known my character in the least bit."

"Yes, I faltered, but I do know your character. I know that you haven't broken your vows."

"How could you possibly know that? You weren't here. You left. You know nothing of my life. You chose not to be in it."

"Have you?"

The question stumped her, because the answer was no. It had been a point of pride, refusing to even consider anything that would break her vows.

"The only reason you say so now is because someone else has confirmed to you that I didn't. It's the only reason you're here. Someone else's word. Not mine. You were quite happy to condemn me a mere week back."

"I'm sorry."

"You're sorry," she said with a snort. "What good is that to me?"

"And I am sorry we are in this position. I take full responsibility."

This was all getting too much for her. She couldn't bear any more, so she walked past him to the door.

"Eliza," he called, but she refused to listen. "I did this. And I will bear the consequences."

"What consequences?" she demanded, her anger reasserting itself again. "What possible consequences are there for you?"

"I will not force your hand in anything, so we will have the kind of relationship you deem for us to have. Even if you completely ignore your vows and take… lovers."

Anger and sadness were fighting so fiercely inside her, she couldn't get anything out. "You are quite the martyr, aren't you, Caius?" she spat and fled as fast as she could before the tears came. Because if the tears came, he would probably try to comfort her and she would probably... hit him. "Then we will have nothing!" she yelled back, not even sure he heard.

But no, they would not be picking up the pieces where they'd left off. And no, she wasn't going to be dictated to by him. As far as she was concerned the ending of their marriage was already a done thing. If he wouldn't give her a divorce, she would act as if he had. This was not... tolerable.

In her distress, she'd left the building and was walking randomly, just getting further and further away from him and the mess he'd caused. Well, at least he acknowledged he'd caused it. And he was still causing it. Part of her had to wonder if he was doing this to hurt her. No, it wasn't like him. This was conviction for him. They did not have just cause for divorce, so they wouldn't divorce. But then to say that they would still be married even if she took a lover. That... that was punishing them both for his stupid mistakes.

Why did he have to be so impossible?

For a moment, she wondered if it was possible to find William Castle Garrick and have him convince Caius it was true. Surely the man couldn't be so intent on telling the truth now. Lying hadn't bothered him the least little bit before.

How she wished Teresa was here so she could talk to someone about it. The truth was that she didn't have many friends. Largely she had stayed away from people and the awkward questions about where her husband was and why she was living in Lambeth running a business in what was an unladylike fashion.

Another dark thought occurred to her. She really would be Lady Warwick if Caius refused to divorce her. A prospect she absolutely didn't want as it would only draw more attention to her. It was one thing being the wife of a military officer, who was away for lengthy periods of time, quite another to be the separated wife of a titled gentleman with both of them in the same city.

This was all unbearable, but Caius had told her in no uncertain terms that bear it they would. Even if separated and living separate lives.

No, this was his impetuousness speaking. Guilt fueling him now, but in the long term, he would want a family and an heir, and it could be that he would be much more open to the logic of divorcing when his shock of his guilt subsided. Emotions drove these decisions, and those emotions would pass.

In six months, he might feel very differently.

The thought soothed her. None of this was set in stone. His determination that her lack of real guilt with regards to adultery could change too. It might well be that he would be amenable to looking over recent questions raised with regards to the William Castle Garrick scandal. It was the perfect excuse for divorce. It was well known and it was shocking. Clear grounds for divorce—if Caius could just get over his squeamishness about some wobbly facts.

No, that is what they would do. Caius needed time to process things. This was all in the heat of the moment for him and he was making bad decisions. Given time, he would calm down and they could get everything back on track. The divorce track that was. Not the silly track he was proposing.

Chapter 23:

FOR A MOMENT, CAIUS wondered if he could bar the door when he saw his father's carriage pull up. Octavia would pry. It is what she always did and Caius wasn't in the mood to talk about anything.

"Sister," he said when Mr. Jones helped her in. They embraced and it felt nice to have her there—nice to have family there.

Why were all his emotions contradicting each other right now? Black and white at the same time.

"How are you?"

How could he possibly answer that question? "Well. As you see."

"And how are things with Eliza?"

Direct to the point. That was his sister. "Yes, I have seen her."

"And what does she say?"

"Would you like some refreshment? You must be parched after your journey. Come through to the salon."

There was nothing Mr. Jones hated more than having to do tea service for ladies. Nothing pushed the man as far out of his comfort zone as ladies. They tended to confound the man with the things they said and asked for. At no point had Mr. Jones ever known any ladies and he hadn't a clue how to handle them, and Octavia wasn't easy for her own family to handle.

"Don't change the subject, Caius."

"We don't have a subject yet. You've barely gotten in the door."

"Well, I am in now and I am seated."

"Fine, she did not take it well."

"Take what well?"

"The fact that we are not divorcing."

Octavia was quiet, her eyes searching his. "I see. No doubt you made a hash of it."

"No doubt," he confirmed. "All in all, I can't say things are going swimmingly. Quite clearly, she doesn't like me and I don't think she is all that keen on this marriage continuing."

"Are you keen on the marriage continuing?"

"I think we owe our vows to continue, but from a certain perspective, one could say that vows are already broken."

"You mean from her perspective," Octavia added, taking a sip of her tea. "So now what? Are you to order her to Bickerley like some ogre?"

"No, of course not."

"But you want a reconciliation?"

The question was hard to answer. It was something he'd mentally stayed away from. Because on one hand, he would make himself unhappy if he set himself on it and it didn't happen—if Eliza chose to pursue a life completely apart from him. "I am not sure that's possible."

"But you wish for a marriage that is as it should be?" Octavia pressed.

It annoyed him that she pressed, but knew it was because it was an answer he needed to formulate, one he wasn't sure he was ready to. "Yes. But as I said, I am not sure that it's a realistic desire. I seem to make her cry every time I speak to her." Eliza fought it, but he could see the tears she refused to shed. It was the reason she ran from him just about every time they spoke. Except with the solicitors. Perhaps the only way they could have a prolonged conversation would be with solicitors arbitrating.

"That is a good sign, I think."

"What?"

"That she cries."

"How could that possibly be a good sign?"

"Well, it isn't cool indifference, is it?"

The logic had him stumped for a moment. "So you think there is hope?"

"She fell in love with you once. There is obviously something about you that appeals to her. And with love, I don't think it ever truly goes away. Not if it was real in the first place."

Caius thought back on his first meeting with her after returning from the Orient. No, it had twisted his gut. As much as he'd wanted cool indifference, emotions had burned through his blood. Neither of them were indifferent, and according to Octavia that was a good sign. "I'm not sure she would hear out any suggestion I put to her in that regard. She is angry with me. Deeply so. She feels I failed her as a husband, and it is hard to argue that I didn't."

"Then you must convince her that you will not fail her again."

"I doubt she'll listen."

"I suppose that is where you will have to get creative, brother. If you cannot, then perhaps you don't deserve to have her back."

"It is always so pleasant when you come visit."

"You do not like it that I give you the plain facts."

"Perhaps it is the brutal way in which you deliver them," he said with a smile. "But why are you here? Did you come simply to witness this debacle, or are you here for a reason?"

"I am, as it happens," she said. "I thought it was timely I spend some time with my friends. Particularly as myself and Terence Elkwood have had a falling out."

"Terence Elkwood doesn't fall out with anyone." Caius said, remembering the young man from his school days. Hadn't seen him in years.

"No, he does, when it suits him. Also has the capacity to be pigheaded."

"Right," Caius said, starting to realize that this was perhaps an issue he shouldn't get involved with. His sister had always been perfectly able to fight her own battles, and if Terence Elkwood was about to head into battle with her, then Caius felt sorry for him.

He had his own battle to worry about and no idea what strategies he could use. This was unknown territory. His courtship with Eliza had been so easy. His interest had been clear from the moment he'd seen her and she had reciprocated in the same easy way. Spending time with her had been fun and he'd grown more fond of her every time he'd seen her, until the day when he just couldn't wait to see her. Planning ways to spend time with her had been all-consuming. They'd gotten engaged and then married.

Maybe there was some old wives' tale that said a courtship that was so easy would spell a troubled marriage, because that was the best way to describe what they'd had.

So how in the world would he court her again? It would definitely not be as easy as calling at her parents' house. In fact, she would probably bar him entry if he called at her house now. Likely she'd barred him entry into her business as well, and he would have to accost her on the street, where they tended to end up yelling at each other, like unruly street urchins.

If he invited her, she would probably not come—even to a meeting planned with the solicitors. Nothing according to the typical means of engagement would appeal to her and she could simply say no. There was nothing she wanted from him other than his absence.

But he wouldn't give up on this marriage that easily. Because it was a very good marriage—had been a very good marriage, until he'd made a total hash of it.

So what did she want? The one thing she was focused on was her business. The brute's way would be to hold it to ransom, but he couldn't deploy such tactics. There had to be gentler tactics.

Octavia's chatter broke into his thoughts. "But I would appreciate it if you could escort me to the Sanderson party."

"What?"

"The Sanderson party. I need an escort."

"But I don't wish to go to parties." Unless there was some way of getting Eliza there. Unfortunately, she had little interest in parties. Although she would be interested if it helped her business. Which the Sanderson party wouldn't do. But there were others that did. Things he could open up for her. Connections he could make.

It all hinged on if her desire to advance her business was stronger than her desire to avoid him.

"Are you not hearing a single word I am saying? Will you please take me."

"Yes, fine," he agreed, primarily to stop her pestering, which she was supremely good at when there was something she wanted. Perhaps a quality he needed to cultivate. Or not. It was hard to tell what tactics were needed. This wasn't something he'd ever done before. It was unchartered territory, but the prize was worth every effort.

Chapter 24:

TO ELIZA IT FELT A LITTLE like she'd veered completely off course, and she had no influence over it. In reality, it was the same course she'd been on the whole time, married to an absent husband, getting on with her business. And there was no threat to the business now that there was no divorce, but she'd gotten used to the idea of being divorced, had planned for it.

It would have been devastating in many ways, but she had planned for that, had anticipated it. But it also had some opportunities—one of possibly finding someone to share her time with again. It might have been too much to hope for a new husband, but to be free of her vows—that had been something both scary and thrilling.

Now that wasn't to be. And yes, technically he was right, because she had never broken her vows. He might have—she would never ask—but that wasn't grounds for divorce in a man's case. They had no grounds for divorce, but that didn't mean they couldn't go ahead and divorce. The opportunity was there, so why was he refusing to take it? Because it hadn't been true.

Neither had her scandal with William Castle Garrick, but he'd jumped on that opportunity.

She'd been so angry with him that she'd yelled at him. In no uncertain terms had she told him what she felt about him. So it couldn't be that he held delusions about that. A poor excuse for a husband. Partially, she'd said it to convey to him that they should continue with the divorce, because she wasn't interested in staying married to him. She deserved a better husband, or no husband.

One of the clerks came in and placed a bundle of envelopes on her desk and she smiled tightly in thanks as he retreated.

And Caius had said the ball was in her court now. It was just a matter of time and they would see if her wish for freedom would outweigh his wish for an heir. Granted he was a young man and he had time. He had time to wait.

What was she going to do? What could she do? She had no power or say in this thing. All she could do was get on with it.

Leaning over, she grabbed the bundle of mail and went through it. Bills and requests, pausing when she saw Caius' handwriting. There was a distinctive flourish he used when he wrote her name and she knew it immediately. Frowning, she stared at it. What now?

For a moment she wanted to put it back and forget it was there, but that would do no good whatsoever. With a sigh, she cracked the seal and unfolded the parchment.

Dear Wife, it started and a small growl escaped her lips, because she didn't like him referring to her that way. It felt as if it was a right he'd given up when he'd refused to believe her.

As I mentioned, I do take responsibility for the failings in our marriage. I have taken to heart your charge that

I did not support you when you needed it. Unfortunately, that is true.

And while our marriage might not be something you value these days, I find I can support you in the endeavors you do value.

I have in my time become acquainted with Lord Sunderstone. I believe you must be familiar with who he is, but in case you are not, he chairs the commission in charge of the workhouses across England. As your interest is to supply charity schools with quality educational material, I anticipate it would be an ambition of yours to get your educational materials into the workhouse schools.

While I may not be able to undo the past, I can help with your hopes and ambitions for the future. Let me know if this is something of interest and I can arrange a meeting.

My Deepest Regard,

Caius

Placing the letter down on her desk, Eliza stared at it. Getting her material into the workhouses would be quite a coup. It had been her intention from the very start that the material she created would be available to all children, particularly those who had so little to assist them with their education.

And so far, she'd only met blocks any time she had tried to get in contact with the committee that managed the provisions to the workhouses. So many felt that educational materials were unnecessary, particularly as the workhouse schools focused so much on trade skills. Little was spared for more general education, especially for younger children, when a trade like domestic service was far more important than learning to read and write.

A chance to meet and discuss her materials with Lord Sunderstone would allow her to explain how important it was and how her materials would help. It was too important an opportunity to pass up. But why would Caius want to help her like this? What did he hope to achieve by it?

Perhaps it was guilt that made him offer this. What other agenda could he possibly have? It wasn't as if he wanted something from her like he had when he'd sought her guilty plea for the divorce. Unless he saw this as some means for rekindling their relationship. He had alluded to something to that effect during their last discussion, which was more an episode of her yelling at him. She wasn't proud of it, but they were things she'd needed to say.

Or perhaps he simply wanted a more cordial relationship between them, which wasn't surprising considering their last meeting.

Whatever the reason for him doing this, it was too much of an opportunity to pass up. She would have to accept it, even if the offer made her wary.

How she wished Teresa was here to advise her how to deal with this. Although Teresa's advice was a little harsh at times. Her opinion of men and marriage was quite firmly eroded by her experiences.

No perhaps it was best that Teresa was not here to advise her right now. Reaching over, she pulled a piece of paper over and picked up her pen to accept Caius' offer. This opportunity would go a long way to achieve the goals of this company, and it would greatly benefit the most needy children in the country, who would be much better off with the education she wanted to bring to them. The whole country would be better off. A worthy goal indeed.

All it required was for her to accept her 'husband's' assistance. It felt odd calling him her husband. In the short time he had been back and they'd headed toward divorce, she had stopped thinking of him as such. Instead, he'd become the adversary she'd tried to stop thinking about.

Whatever purpose this was for, or whatever discomfort it would bring her, even if she had to show gratitude, she would do it. It was a worthy cause and it far outweighed her concerns.

The wax sealed the envelope and she asked one of the young men who performed whatever errands were needed within the company to deliver the letter to Lord Warwick's address.

Surely it would be a simple meeting after a written introduction. In truth, she wasn't even sure where the commission for the workhouses sat. It could well be in Parliament itself, or one of the attached buildings. After the meeting, she would write a thank you letter to Caius saying she appreciated his assistance. She just wasn't sure what he expected in return, because she didn't know what she was willing to give him anything in return. Gratitude might be as far as her appreciation would go. Maybe she would have put something eluding to that in her letter. She hadn't thought of it at the time.

Chapter 25:

"LORD SUNDERSTONE IS in Devon," Caius said when he put down the letter he'd just received. "He says we are welcome to join the party to visit him."

"A visit," Octavia said, slowly clinking the small teaspoon against the fine bone china of her teacup. "How nice."

"Says he is going to France after, so it is unlikely Eliza can see him for a while."

"Unless you take her to the house party. She might enjoy a jaunt in the country."

"I doubt she will enjoy it in my company."

"I suppose that depends on how badly she wants to meet this man."

Caius considered it. "We could spend the day yelling at each other."

"She will if she wants to make a good impression on this man, hence would be on her best behavior. If you do wish to spend some time with her, this would be the perfect opportunity."

That was true. A trip to Devon would keep them in close, cramped proximity for hours on end. It would give them the chance to talk, more than just yelling at each other. Although there could be that too. "She will perceive it as manipulative."

"Yes, and how is that an issue? She is your wife. You can either let her take charge of this relationship, or you can do so. What is so horrible about you stacking things in your favor? And while you are there, Lord Sunderstone will probably expect her to act as a wife would."

"I cannot ask her to do that." Octavia was implying that Lord Sunderstone would expect man and wife to share a room.

"Brother, if you are to put this right, then you must be a little manipulative. Or you could be waiting a century for her to feel sorry enough for you to forgive you."

Is that what it would take, her feeling sorry for him?

"As they say," Mr. Jones cut in, "all is fair in love and war."

Caius certainly knew all was fair in war, but was the same thing true now? Should he use this opportunity to get what he wanted? Which was what exactly?

The answer wasn't hard to uncover—to get his wife back. Whatever affections she had for this Lord Fortescue, he needed to steal her away. Or else she might continue down a track that didn't serve his ends at all. Even if he'd said that he would accept whatever relationship she deemed suitable for them, it didn't mean he couldn't influence it.

And Octavia seemed to think that pity was the way to crack Eliza's heart. Not that there was anything particularly pitiful about him. Well, other than he'd destroyed his relationship with his wife based on the lies of a man he'd thought had been a friend. In certain light, that could be deemed as Shakespearean levels of tragedy.

But then, he was responsible for not believing her, so how could he be pitied?

Checking his fob watch, he saw it was time to leave. "I must go."

"Are you sure you don't want to come?" he asked Octavia.

"And watch you moon over your wife for days on end. No, thank you. Besides, I have my own battle to deal with."

"This is not battle."

"Yes, it is. And if you're not careful, it will be your blood on the ground."

Shaking his head, Caius rose. He didn't entirely prescribe to Octavia's view of the world, or of relationships, but perhaps she was right in the sense that he and Eliza were at odds, and they had to find a way forward, either in the direction he wanted, or the one she wanted.

It was time to leave and Caius made his way out to the carriage. A trunk had been loaded in the back and he felt a tinge of oddness thinking that Eliza's would join his. It seemed such a mundane thing, but Eliza's things hadn't joined his in a very long time.

The driver had already been informed of the destination and made his way through the traffic leading to the Westminster Bridge. With each mile, the tension in him rose. Technically it wasn't far between their houses, but they were very different areas, and the streets became much harder to navigate as soon as they crossed the bridge, until they arrived at her small townhouse, in what was seemingly a respectable street for the neighborhood.

As he opened the carriage door to step out, Eliza emerged from her door. "I hadn't realized this would be such an undertaking when I agreed." There was tartness in her voice. She wasn't pleased.

"It is the only way, I'm afraid. Lord Sunderstone is off to France and you wouldn't get a chance to see him again for quite some time. Besides, he would look more favorably on a proposition given to him in his own home than a presentation in some office."

They stood facing each other for a moment, while the driver organized her things to join his. "Lady Warwick."

Her jaw tightened in response. She didn't like being referred to either as a lady, or as his lady. Still, she had to know that the title would be expected during the visit.

For a moment, it looked like she would refuse his hand to assist her as well, but she relented. Her hand was warm in his, slight and soft, unlike his rough and calloused ones. He assisted her, but he wanted to not let go once inside, but he did as he got in himself. Then they were on their way.

It was a different atmosphere in the carriage with her presence. Both comforting and precarious. Her eyes watched out the window as the streets passed by. She said very little.

How beautiful she was. The beauty that had so captivated him when he'd met her. He'd seen her and he'd known she would be meaningful to him. Then for many years he'd cursed that beauty.

Chapter 26:

SITTING WITH CAIUS LIKE this was uncomfortable and painful. But maybe this was her fault for being so ambitious. Still, a chance to reach all those children, the most needy children in the country was worth personal discomfort.

And it wasn't as if she thought Caius was lying to her. He wasn't. It was just that words were easy. But equally, he didn't simply want a cordial relationship between them—he wanted reconciliation, even if he wouldn't blatantly say it.

While she may have said all the things in her heart, as he'd suggested, she still couldn't let go of the feelings—the anger. As much as she wanted to rage, she'd said the things she thought about him and about the whole debacle that had been their marriage. Was their marriage. They were still married, unfortunately, and he saw no justifiable reason for that to change.

Lady Warwick. She was now in a position to have to embrace the title. For the children. It was worth it for the children.

In a way, her mind was exhausted, but she couldn't escape Caius in this small carriage. Even with her eyes closed, she felt his presence. And she couldn't let herself look at him, because so many emotions still lay just underneath the surface, threatening to emerge.

"How is your sister?" she asked, as a means to distract from her own thoughts.

"Well. I saw her this morning. She is set on dressing down some man who has upset her."

"I expect she would be good at that." Eliza knew what it felt like enduring Octavia's displeasure. The woman had a means of making one feel like an offending worm. Judging by how harshly Octavia had reacted during the scandal, she would hardly be pleased by Caius' decision not to go ahead with the divorce, or did she also think that vows should be kept even if a total hash had been made of the relationship. "Poor man." Silence descended again. Conversation was so awkward between them. "Your family must be glad you are back."

"They are." Although with his brother it was debatable. There was a competitiveness between them that they'd never been able to overcome. Octavia was the peacemaker in the family, and if she married, she might take her mediation skills as such with her. "Families come with their own strains."

"Better than being without."

"I concur with your sentiment. One should never truly give up on family." A stain colored her cheeks, because she understood the reference. And she was getting tired of reminder them both that he had given up on them as family. "But being in the Orient had its benefits."

"Such as?" she asked, unable to stop herself being drawn into the conversation. Caius looked pleased with her engagement in the conversation.

"The Eastern cultures are very different. Fascinating in some respect. History weighs heavily on their thinking. Sometimes in our own, I wonder if we consider it enough."

"What do you mean?"

"I don't know. In my experience, we often seem to make the same mistake over again. Stay anywhere long enough and you will see people repeat things that never worked well for them."

"Like us?"

"Well, as I recall, we worked supremely well together, before the mistake that I refuse to make again."

A frown drew her brow together. "You believe we can rekindle," she said.

"I do believe we can. I even believe we should. If we will is another thing altogether. The fundamentals of our relationship are still there, are they not? We had a good marriage, we worked well together. The distance between us is not related to us being unsuitable at the most basic level."

"That does not mean we should be together."

"You mean that you should not forgive me."

"It's not that simple," she said in a stronger tone. He was trying her temper, because he was forcing her to talk about things she didn't want to talk about, maybe even to think about.

"Nothing ever is. It is just that in my time away from here, I have learned what is worth fighting for."

She bit her lips together and her eyes returned to the window. On some level, she didn't agree. Perhaps because she was still so angry with him, and he was oversimplifying everything that had happened..

"So who is this woman you are living with?" he asked

"Teresa, and her children. You met one of them, if you recall."

"Honestly, I was so irrational, I don't really recall much."

Her attention came back to him, and his eyes seemed to draw her back. "Well, you terrified the child."

"Honestly, I gave myself pause too. I don't normally react that way. Your actions, real or perceived, have a way of... piercing."

"Well, I found Teresa huddling in the street with her children. She'd fled her husband, and I'd been discarded by mine. As it happened, I was huddling slightly less than she, so I invited her to stay. It turned out to suit both of us. I asked her to come work in the business, and largely we run it together. We share an understanding in that regard."

"How so?"

"That women should support one another, particularly when no one else can be depended on. Also perhaps in the firm belief that we should invest in our children, no matter what their background. It is unjust that we ignore some children in our society."

"A noble cause. Then I am glad I can assist you with it."

"But also to serve your own purposes."

He smiled. "It truly is the only way to see Lord Sunderstone, but I will not pretend I am displeased. It gives us the opportunity to get to know each other again, the people we are now."

The conversation drifted and he let it fall silent.

"It has been a while since I've left London," she finally said. "Certainly not by carriage."

"Because of the location of Lord Sunderstone's estate, the rail lines are inconvenient. But I understand there are plans to build rail out that way."

"It is transforming the country," Eliza said. "It truly is transforming the means and ease of travel."

"Quite a few things have changed. You notice after returning from a long absence."

They chatted amiably about things that had changed. Eliza wasn't relishing the conversation, but she participated, and he even made her smile on a few occasions. It was much easier to discuss things that didn't specifically pertain to either of them.

With weariness, she wondered if they would slip into easy conversation again. Perhaps this was a part of his plan, or on the other side, it was easier to talk of rail developments than about them.

Then the conversation died for a while and Eliza sat with her eyes closed. It wasn't a nap as such, but more a rest. It was something she liked to do when she traveled. It also gave her a way to escape his scrutiny, and provided a means for their conversation not to become too easy.

“I believe there is an inn not too far ahead.” Both of them would benefit from stretching their legs a bit, and a moment away from such nearness.

In all honestly, Eliza wasn't sure how she felt about a visit to a country house. They were designed for intimate groups of friends, wiling away hours in each other's company. Social gatherings had been very low on her priority for years, and she hadn't missed them a bit. Now she found them uncomfortable and awkward. Also she wondered if her complete focus on business these years had made her unsuited to such activities. But she had to traverse this unpleasantness to achieve her goal.

For a moment, she studied Caius as he wasn't looking at her when she opened her eyes. His face had changed a little, become broader. His time away had changed him, had changed his demeanor. There was a heaviness in him, which was probably a good part due to his guilt and unhappiness of the state of things. But she had a feeling it was more than that, more than them. He'd had experiences that had changed him too, had been to war, had seen things that the man she had known hadn't.

But then she had changed too, and she prided herself on that as opposed to being devastated by her reduced circumstances, she had flourished. She felt as if she had done well for herself. She was proud of her achievements without him, and she now knew she could handle anything that was thrown at her.

Now she had to deal with him and she was curious to see how she would do so.

He would push and she would push back. Still, she remembered the time where there had been no pushing between them, when they'd come together like it was the most natural thing in the world. Memories she didn't want encroaching now. They didn't suit her purposes.

Quickly, she closed her eyes so he would not catch her studying him.

Chapter 27:

THE GENTLE KNOCK ON the roof drew Eliza out of her half slumber. Caius wanted to stop. Opening her eyes, she tried to orient herself for a moment.

"We're approaching the inn. I thought we could both use some refreshment."

"Right," she said and straightened in her seat, trying to rid herself of her sleepiness. The hoof falls, the gentle swaying of the carriage, it had all been quite lulling, and she'd likely be fully asleep soon if they weren't stopping.

The carriage pulled to a stop outside the inn. A brick building with flowers planted under the windows. It looked respectable enough.

Caius stepped down onto the gravel and turned to assist her. In some ways, she wanted to refuse his help, but it would stir more attention than it was worth. Even if they were strangers, he was bound to assist her. Perhaps it was that she didn't like touching him. He wore no gloves, but she did, and she was grateful for it. Because in her gut, she knew he would take as much as she was prepared to give.

The inn was quiet, but they weren't the only people there as they walked in. There were tables of different sizes, some were occupied, while others weren't. The dark wood contrasted with white walls.

The proprietor approached, wearing a clean apron, which was comforting to see.

"Are you hungry?" Caius asked, as they searched for a suitable seat, taking one over in the corner by the window.

"The Mrs. has just pulled out some scones from the oven," the man said jovially. "They do smell lovely if I say so myself," he finished and Eliza's mouth watered even thinking about fresh scones coming out of the oven.

"With some tea, please," she added.

"And I will come peruse your selection of tipple."

"This way," the man said, leading him to the serving bar, where a couple of men stood, quietly partaking in their ales.

Caius was searching for whiskey, a habit he seemed not to have lost. An interest she didn't understand, but she supposed she appreciated his consistency with it.

Before long, he returned with a glass of golden liquid. "Anything interesting?"

"He had an Irish I've never tried," he said when he sat down. "I do like the Irish."

"I think you like all of them."

"They all have different features. This one is a little sharper. Another few years and it would settle down nicely. Not that it's bad."

"You should build your own cellar and wait for them to age."

"Yes, but unfortunately my uncle's cellar is full of wine."

Throughout the time she'd known him, he'd never been as enthusiastic about wine as he was about whiskey, or anything else for that matter. "Throw a house party and they'll drink your wine cellar dry."

"Ugh, I'd have to have people over."

"You used to be quite enthusiastic about house parties."

"Once upon a time. It has been a long time since I've attended country parties. Much less hosted any. Honestly I think I'm more wary of this house party than you are."

Eliza hadn't been aware her wariness was quite so noticeable. He'd obviously observed it, or the assumption was not peculiar under the circumstances.

The proprietor returned with a tray carrying a teapot and a basket of scones, a small pot of jam and a portion of butter. It smelled lovely, bringing back childhood memories. Why had it been so long since she'd eaten a scone? Because it had been a while since she'd had lazy days indulging in treats.

With the knife she cut one in half and smeared on butter, which melted with the warmth. Like this, she actually preferred them savory, so she forwent the jam and stuck with butter. They tasted lovely.

Caius watched her and she blushed. "Would you like one?"

"I might. In a moment."

"Don't take too long, or they will cool."

With a smile, he raised his glass to his lips and sipped.

"Will you not miss your commission?"

"No," he said without doubt. "Maybe. I don't know yet. Some parts perhaps, others not at all. I won't miss any of it sufficiently that I would wish to undo coming back. I have seen some amazing things, and I have seen things I wish I hadn't."

His expression told her he was earnest. A part of her felt she should be responsible, but she refused. She hadn't done anything to cause him to take the commission.

"So now you are to settle down and be a gentleman farmer?"

"In essence."

"What if it doesn't suit you?"

"Then I will not fare well. One must find ways of making it suit. Could you imagine no way of living if you didn't have your business?"

"We would be substantially worse off if we didn't."

"You would be intent on refusing my assistance, then?"

This was not the conversation she wished to have. "Your assistance, over the years, has been very helpful."

"It was also spiteful."

"I never saw it that way."

"I could have afforded to keep you better."

"You could have not kept me at all."

Caius reached for one of the scones and gently tore it in half. With the knife, he spread jam on it and savored it. "Our past is a tale of woe," he finally said. "I think we can both agree. I suppose what remains to be seen is how the future will be. I think neither of us wants a similar future."

"The future," she said absently, not understanding what her emotions were right then. "Truthfully, I have been more concerned with the here and now than I have with the future."

"I can say the same. But now I find I have to consider the future. So does Lord Fortescue, I would think."

Eliza had known this would come up at some point, and now they were having this conversation. She was curious what he would say. "I cannot possibly say."

"I think it takes a man with intention to visit a lady during illness."

"You did." She knew she was deflecting the conversation back, because she didn't want to talk about Lord Fortescue and how curious she had been about him. Still was to some degree, but Caius refusing to divorce her was changing things in that regard. How, she wasn't sure yet. She wasn't sure how she felt, or what she wanted for her future. For a while, she'd seen potential with Lord Fortescue, but did she see it the same now that Caius refused to end their marriage? It was a question she'd been avoiding.

"The need to tend to you returned," he said.

"Your intentions were quite firmly to divorce me at that point."

"I learned you were sick and I rushed to find you." Color was creeping up her cheeks. These revelations were uncomfortable.

"And found someone else had rushed ahead of you. I gather you presumed he was my paramour."

"I knew he wasn't."

"You knew he wasn't, but you didn't know Rosie wasn't my child, let alone yours."

"I was irrational, and it was fairly easy to establish that Lord Fortescue wasn't your lover."

"How did you establish that?"

"Your manner and distance said so."

"And you have also said you will not interfere if that changes."

A tight smile ghosted across his lips. "I did." His words said so, but his expression said he wouldn't be quite so welcoming of the development. "I am not sure either of us will find it so easy to put aside our marriage vows."

Was he trying to guilt her into not considering Lord Fortescue? "In that case I don't think you entirely understand the status of our relationship."

"Perhaps. But as angry as I was, when you needed me, I came running."

"But I didn't need you."

"Clearly," he said tartly. "But dropping everything to find you felt like the only rational thought I'd had since the moment I stepped foot on English soil. Every emotion I had ignored for years all returned, but when I worried for you, it all melted away."

"And you assume I would come running if you were ill in return?"

"No, perhaps not, but I am not sure that matters."

"It should matter. As far as I'm concerned you're the one that broke the marriage vows. Nowhere in the vows we made did it say we should desert each other if we were disappointed, or if unscrupulous persons cast accusations. And you have promised me that you will not interfere with the decisions I make."

"That is true. But I am only voicing what I feel. Simply the truth. Do you wish for me to lie to you?"

"No."

"Then we agree to tell the truth, no matter what it means."

Nerves clenched deep in her stomach. "I have never not told the truth."

"Then we continue in that fashion."

"Fine," she agreed.

Chapter 28:

ANGRY SILENCE EMANATED from Eliza throughout the rest of the carriage ride. Exactly what she was angry about, he couldn't pinpoint. There were so many things she was angry about and he couldn't blame her.

Toward dusk, they were turning into the road that led to the Sunderstone estate, lined with trees, leading to a large house with neat rows of windows and a jumble of chimneys. The parklands extended far and a manicured garden surrounded the house. Not one for informal and romantic gardens, it seemed. More influenced by the French.

"It's a magnificent house," she said, looking out the window.

"I think you would like Bickerley Hall." In their time together, she'd met his uncle, but never visited Bickerley.

Sitting back in her seat, she didn't respond for a moment. "How do you feel about inheriting it?"

"I suppose I always knew I would, but it was still a shock when it happened. But as for the house, it's lovely. It needs some repairs, but it's been well managed."

Saying that, he wanted to invite her to come see it, but knew she wouldn't be welcoming of such an invitation right at this point, but maybe that would change.

The carriage came to the house and the deep gravel crunched under the wheels as they drew closer. A retainer came to greet them and it felt like a blessing to leave the carriage behind, but he could tell that Eliza was nervous. She'd been away from this kind of company for six years, and so had he. "I'm afraid we might both be a little rusty when it comes to etiquette," he said as they walked up to the house. "And unknowing for any of the current iterations."

"Yes," she agreed.

The house was sumptuous, more elaborately decorated than the houses in his family. The white curved staircase had marble statues along it and a glass dome over the entrance hall. The Sunderstone family had built a house to impress. A house told a great deal about the cares and ambitions of a family, and the Sunderstone family wanted to impress.

"His lordship is in the parlor," the man said, taking their accompaniments and directing the way.

They walked into a thickly carpeted room with silk-covered walls. It was warm and a number of people were present. It occurred to him that he should have gotten Eliza a better dress, but it hadn't entered his mind. Mostly because she looked stunning as she was. Even so, it wasn't a dress to the standard displayed here.

"Ah," Lord Sunderstone said and came over. "Lord Warwick, such a pleasure you could join us. And this is your wife. We haven't met. I believe I would remember such a beauty."

The man considered her as Caius introduced them and a spear of jealousy hit him. Not at Lord Sunderstone's regard, but more at the sweet nothings Lord Fortescue was probably whispering in her ear. An urge to bundle her up and hide her clawed through him, but it was unreasonable and irrational. There was that irrationality that only she brought out of him.

"I am pleased to make your acquaintance, and thank you for inviting us to your marvelous home," Eliza said with a smile. This wasn't the Eliza he knew. This was the proprietress of her business in action. It was the reason they were here.

She kept her assured smile as they were introduced to all in the party, and he certainly didn't need to interfere with her charm in introducing herself. Eliza knew exactly what to do and how she wanted these people to perceive her. These were her customers.

"Now, my dear Lady Warwick, do you play cards. I'm not sure I dare play with your husband. I suspect he might fleece me."

"Caius does have a way with cards," she said and gave him a look before she walked over to the card table with their host, leaving Caius to regret finding himself alone in this room. The invitation in some of the women's eyes were a little too strong and he retreated to converse with a man he didn't know, who turned out to be Lord Sunderstone's cousin, Harold Marsham, who was inordinately interested in the geological history of Britain, it turned out.

Well, that should teach him to approach the man no one else talked to. Often there was a reason, but the conversation gave him ample opportunity to drift his attention away to watch Eliza, who was charming Lord Sunderstone.

One truth he had to face was that as opposed to what he said, he couldn't tolerate Lord Fortescue buzzing around her, and he even contemplated rough means of chasing him away. His years in the military had introduced some forceful ways of dealing with people. Had seen them utilized more than done so himself, but in this case, he might make an exception.

"Lord Warwick," a woman said, approaching them. "I believe we met some years ago. Josephine Wellsted."

"Yes, of course, a pleasure to see you again," he said and kissed the hand she extended. "How is Richard?"

"Well as I understand it. He's in Egypt at the moment, but it's too hot there right now for me to join him."

"Yes, I understand the summer months can be uncomfortable."

"We are so pleased you could join us. It has been some time since you've been seen in society. I understand you have been out serving the benefits of the empire. Did your wife join you?"

"No, unfortunately. Although, she tends to focus quite heavily on her charitable work when I'm away."

"Oh," the woman said as if that was unusual. It was unusual. Everything about their relationship was unusual, but they had to make it sound perfectly reasonable. "Quite the beauty, isn't she?"

"Yes," he agreed.

"One has to say that time apart does make the heart grow fonder. I find I miss my Richard inordinately when he's away. I am quite sure we would have gotten bored of each other by now otherwise."

Getting bored of Eliza wasn't something he could imagine, but he hadn't allowed himself to miss her for a moment he'd been gone, and he'd been quite successful at blocking her from his mind. It had been necessary, he suspected.

It grew dark quickly and supper was being served. The butler who'd let them in directed them into the dining room, which was white with soaring ceilings. An ornate chandelier hung from the ceiling. No expense had been spared on this room, but Caius saw no reason why he would consider redecorating Bickerley. Nothing in him sought to make the kind of impression Lord Sunderstone did.

Likely that expanded to his charity work. Caius expected it was done for the impression rather than any real concern for the people in his care. It was a point that might put Eliza at odds with the man, because her care was for the children, but then the proposition had the benefits of being impressive. Educating children was an accolade this man would like to claim, so perhaps there was no reason to worry.

Eliza sat across from him. Harriet Benkworth sat to his right and Jasper Partridge to his left. The table accommodated twelve people, so there were quite a few at this party. It seemed not everyone had been present in the parlor when they'd arrived.

Lord Sunderstone had plied Eliza with sherry and Caius knew she wasn't used to it. Her drink was now being consumed very slowly and a blush colored her cheeks, and her eyes were glassy. She couldn't possibly look more charming than she did at that moment, his chest actually constricted—a feeling he'd felt before for her, but quite some time ago.

He burned to kiss her, but he couldn't. She wouldn't accept it. But he had gained her favor once, he simply had to do it again. Every moment together was an opportunity.

Unfortunately, Mr. Partridge was curious about his military career and asked him endless questions, but he did notice that Eliza paid attention.

There was definitely hope here, he concluded. Octavia had been right in that Eliza not being indifferent meant there were still feelings there. If only he could stop making her cry. That would be a good start. So, he had to charm her the way she charmed Lord Sunderstone. They both had an objective for this visit. Ideally, they would both be victorious.

The supper went on for hours. It was the main event of this party, but eventually people grew tired of sitting and they returned to the parlor.

Eliza declined any further drinks and he could tell she was growing tired, and it pleased him that she sought him. "Is it too early to retire?"

"Yes," he replied. "A tad. We should stay for at least another half hour. Give them a little more time to get drunk. Then I can inquire about our room."

She nodded and stayed with him, because she had no more conversation in her, and them together like this looked so natural. It even felt natural.

"Now, as I recall, you are a whiskey man," Bertie Colston said as they stood by the fire.

"You have an excellent memory."

The man drew the attention of the butler. "Two whiskeys. Or perhaps I shouldn't assume and should ask if you want one, Lady Warwick."

"No, thank you," she said with a smile. "I leave the whiskey drinking to Caius."

"Wise choice," Bertie countered. "I recall it being said around the pubs in Oxford that he was formidable when it came to consuming alcohol."

"Many years ago."

"Yes, I couldn't function if I drank now as I did then. But what fun we had."

The butler returned with a silver tray with two generous portions in glasses. On taste, Caius knew immediately which distillery it had come from. A nice one, an expensive one, but an uninspiring one. "I am afraid my wife has reached her limit for tonight and we will retire."

Bertie was disappointed, because it seemed he wanted to speak more about their antics at Oxford. Maybe even drink like they were reliving it, and although that would perhaps be entertaining, it didn't align with Caius' objective for being there.

"Goodnight," Eliza said with a smile and took his offered elbow.

Chapter 29:

UNSUCCESSFULLY, SHE TRIED to hide a yawn as they walked up the stairs. This house was almost obscene in its luxury, but Lord Sunderstone had been very kind inviting them. And quite a charming man.

"Does Lord Sunderstone have some idea of why we're here?"

"I did mention something about you wishing to discuss charitable work with him."

Caius seemed to know where their room was. The idea of sharing a room with him was uncomfortable, but she did understand the reasoning. They were here for Lord Sunderstone's agreement and not to provide a spectacle with the state of their marriage. And now that she was here with these people, she fully understood the sentiment. This circle consisted of bored people and a spectacle would be exactly what they wanted to indulge in. So no matter how uncomfortable this was, they would share a room.

They stopped in front of a room and Caius opened the door to a bedroom as sumptuous as the rest of the house. It was large with a fire and thick carpets.

"After you," he said and Eliza felt a moment of nervousness stepping into the room, because getting her alone served Caius' purposes. Exactly what those purposes were, she couldn't pin down, because his opinion seemed to shift from: your life is yours, do as you please, to: it would solve all problems if we were together again.

Perhaps he was getting nostalgic about what had been, and it couldn't be denied that they had been perfect together. And now there was this new guilt descending on her, suggesting that she was the one that was keeping their reunion from happening.

It wasn't as simple as 'oh you were innocent, let's pick up where we left off.' She just couldn't.

Looking around the room, she sought an alternative place she could sleep. There was a settee by the window. It wasn't quite long enough, but it would be sufficiently soft if she curled up. "I can take the sofa," she suggested.

"That is unnecessary. I can be trusted."

For the most part, she knew that was probably true, but she wasn't sure she could sleep with Caius lying next to her. No, she would be more comfortable on the less than comfortable settee. "Uhm," she said, looking at the sofa, while trying to pick her words. "I think I prefer some distance. It has been a long day in quite cramped quarters." And all day being surrounded by his scent, the sounds of his breath, his mere presence.

"In that case, I am quite happy to sleep on the floor by the fire."

"That isn't necessary."

"I suspect you simply won't be warm enough on the settee."

It was a good point. The blanket available probably wasn't thick enough to sleep by the window. It might be sufficient to sleep by the fire.

"I will sleep by the fire, you take the bed," he reiterated.

It was a logical suggestion and she accepted it rather than stand there and argue about it. "Fine, thank you."

Now there was a moment of discomfort, because she needed to undress, and no maid would come tonight as she was with her husband.

Caius took the blanket and one of the pillows. "Believe me, this floor is just as comfortable as a camp cot. I will feel quite at home."

So few times, she'd wondered how things had been for him in whatever far-flung location he'd taken himself to. From the sounds of it, not that luxurious. "How did you live where you were?"

"It differed. There is typically an officers' house where I would have rooms, but sometimes it was in camp with everyone else. Battles are rarely fought at convenient locations. I've often ended up in tiny cabins in ships. So I am used to sleeping in uncomfortable situations."

Listening intently, she watched as Caius undressed, not quite intending to, but he simply started undressing. It was a sight she hadn't seen in so very long. Then she realized that she should probably undress too. While her trunk was there, she chose to sleep in her shift, rather than take it off and pull on her nightgown, because that would mean standing here utterly naked for a moment, and that was not something she wanted.

Caius moved to the dresser, where their possessions had been neatly laid out, including both of their toothbrushes and powder. Caius brushed his teeth and the reminder of what had been hit her so hard, it was like a wall of sadness. They'd been so perfect and it had all been destroyed.

In all honesty, she wasn't sure she could pry her heart open again. It was simply too injured. Turning around, she surveyed the paintings on the walls to distract herself from her thoughts and emotions. A nice landscape scene of a summer garden.

It felt awkward preparing for bed in front of someone, because she felt his presence so keenly. Hurrying, she finished her preparations, then walked over to the bed, where she unbuttoned her dress and hung it over a chair. It was the nicest dress she had, but clearly subpar in this house. A few of the women had thrown her looks she'd clearly understood. How could *she* have been matched with a man like Lord Warwick.

Their admiration of him hadn't gone unnoticed, but he'd shown little interest in them. Maybe he was fully serious with his intent on staying within the confines of his vows. It wasn't something she asked of him, or even wanted, but he hadn't responded at all to those women's flirting, which had made them more ardent.

Sneaking a glance over to where he lay, she saw him stretched out on the floor. His shirt was off and his skin reflected the light of the fire. He was… broader than he'd been, more solid. Soldiering had built him from a youth into a stronger man.

His eyes were closed and he lay with his wrist behind his head, giving her a moment to observe him fully. It was much harder when those eyes were on her. They seemed to see everything. He watched her much more carefully now than he'd used to. He saw everything she did.

For a moment, she wondered if there was anything she could do to change his focus, send him off in a huff. But truthfully she didn't have the stomach for what that would take. And a small part of her liked his attention, and intention. It felt like justification after everything that had been done to her, but it was a juvenile desire. She shouldn't want his attention unless she intended to do something with it, and she didn't have those intentions.

Was it because she didn't trust him? She took a moment to consider him. No, that wasn't it. She didn't believe he would make the same mistake again. Her reticence really didn't have to do with him, it had to do with trusting and loving someone, with making herself utterly vulnerable to them and then being destroyed by it.

It also made her realize that she hadn't intended on giving all of herself to Lord Fortescue. She would hold something back to protect herself, a piece of her heart that would remain untouched, and he didn't deserve that. Maybe over time she would have, she hoped.

Tears threatened when she shifted down between the sheets, but she didn't want to cry here, or have Caius observe it, because he didn't like her crying and would seek to comfort her. And right now, she wasn't sure she could tolerate his care and kindness. She was too tired, too exhausted. These weeks since he'd returned had exhausted her.

It took mere minutes to fall asleep to dreams she couldn't understand. They weren't fearful, they weren't joyous, they were pensive, almost as if she was waiting for something. Then a noise drew her out, startled her awake with the concern that someone was in the room with her.

Her attention honed and she heard someone move. Fear gripped her for a moment, before she remembered her circumstances. Caius. He was here and he was moving. Why?

Half rising, she opened her eyes, finding him sitting in a chair in the corner. "Caius?"

"Go back to sleep," he said, barely louder than a whisper.

"Is the floor too uncomfortable?"

"No, it's fine. Go to sleep."

She sat up fully. "What's the matter?"

"I have dreams," he said. "I never sleep through the night."

"You don't?" That wasn't how he'd used to be. He'd always been a heavy sleeper. Now he had dreams that woke him, every night seemingly. This must be a reaction to the things he'd experienced. Awful things she couldn't imagine. "Would it be better if you slept on the bed? I am prepared to trust your ability to restrain yourself."

A smile spread across his lips, but she could tell he was tired. "No, honestly, it won't make a difference. I did seem to like the swaying of a ship, though. I found that soothing."

"That is perhaps hard to replicate."

"Maybe I should take a commission in the navy." He said it lightly as if it were a joke, but she frowned. So he could gather more awful experiences to plague his dreams? "I will sleep again. I just need some quiet moments. Go back to sleep."

Laying down again, she tucked her hands under her cheek and watched him as he sat in the chair, turning his attention to the fire. What thoughts were he getting lost in?

The urge to comfort him was still there, but if she tried, it would end up somewhere she didn't want to go, and then he would have more than hope to fire his intentions. And once that levy broke, she wasn't sure it could be boarded up again. Then where would she be? In love with a man she didn't want to love. She'd worked so hard to get herself to a state where she wasn't in love with him. She'd bled enough without doing herself new injuries.

Chapter 30:

ELIZA WAS UP BEFORE HIM, which wasn't surprising as he'd been up half the night. Much more awkward when someone was in the room with him. It had been a long time since someone had slept in the room with him. A habit he only indulged in when forced to in the more dire of circumstances.

Her soft feet padded quietly across the room, trying to be quiet. But sleeping in dangerous locations with spies and assassins had made him react to even the slightest noise.

"You don't have to tread softly," he said, but didn't open his eyes. For some reason, it had been a particularly difficult night and he was tired. But moving around, he would shake the tiredness.

"I'm sorry," she said.

"Are you hungry?"

"Actually, I am."

"I am sure Lord Sunderstone will put on a fantastic spread for breakfast. I think entertaining is him in his element."

"He does seem to like having people around. Someone said there was a picnic planned today at some nearby lake."

A picnic with these dreadful people, he thought darkly. There was nothing wrong with them as such, he just wasn't used to people anymore. Barking orders was comfortable, but it didn't suit a place like this. So in a sense, these few days had the benefit of forcing him back into normal discourse with people, although he was much more interested in a picnic for just him and Eliza.

There was a sweetness in thinking of such things for just the two of them. He wanted to show her things, to see the wonder in her face. Some of that wonder had been lost from her and he regretted it.

The sun was creeping in through the window and it looked set to be a clear, warm day. One of the last before the weather turned truly cold. Warm days and cold nights. He liked this season.

"I'll dress and then I'll leave you to. Would you like me to call one of the maids to assist you?"

"I haven't had a maid helping me in a long time. I probably wouldn't know what to do with one, but thank you."

With a nod, he rose from his makeshift bed and stretched, then pulled on his shirt. He'd come back and refresh himself after breakfast, but for right now, he'd give her some time to get ready for the day. And himself a moment to be without her. There had been times during the night when all he'd wanted was to join her in that bed. His hands had itched for her, her softness and warmth.

Leaving the room, he closed the door behind him and made his way downstairs. The servants were busy managing the house and he made his way out into the cool, fresh air and smoked some tobacco. It was a morning ritual that gave him a moment to plan for the day, and today was about Eliza, and the objective of getting them closer to where he wanted to be.

Firstly, he wanted her to be comfortable in his presence, because she wasn't. Secondly, he wanted her to trust him, and she didn't. If those two things were achieved today, then it would be a marvelous day.

The gardeners were out trimming, and in the distance, he saw grooms exercising horses. Coming from where he'd been, it was hard not to see this all as pointless. Gardens and racehorses—things that had no real bearing on life. But then he'd lived with such heightened stakes, it was hard to adjust to life back in England. It was also hard to stop himself from seeing this all as pointless.

Some soldiers could never readjust to civilian life. It was well-known. They came back into the service again and again, and stayed well beyond their usefulness. If he failed at this, he would become one of them. He feared that he'd been ruined that way, left unable to fare again as a civilian.

Walking, he enjoyed the fresh air and solitude for a moment, but breakfast was served soon and Eliza would come downstairs. Someone was moving inside and he wondered if it was her, but it wasn't when he walked in.

Only a few people were awake for breakfast that morning, others likely recuperating from the night before.

Eliza joined him and they ate with the others. Lord Sunderstone arrived and they talked about the arrangements for the day. Carriages had been organized to take them to the lake shortly after breakfast concluded.

To Caius, a picnic seemed like the most inane thing one could do, but it was a day with Eliza, which was exactly what he wanted. And it was to his benefit that she didn't connect well with the women there, because if she did, she'd need him much less then.

The wind had warmed considerably by the time they made it out to the carriages and it took yet another half hour for everyone to find a seat. Mustering ladies was a whole different affair than mustering soldiers, and he couldn't yell at them—as much as he wanted to.

"I think we are both uncomfortable in this company," he said.

"At least you are welcome. I am not," she replied. "I think they see me as a poor excuse for a lady."

"Yet you are Lady Warwick."

It was hard to pin her eyes and read her thoughts. She was being brave for being here, and he did feel a little guilty for her discomfort being to his benefit.

It was a lovely drive, though, and they arrived at an idyllic looking lake, with trees surrounding it, reeds growing close to the shore and a grassy area. Even swans serenely swam across the still water.

"Oh, it's lovely," Eliza stated, and Caius swore he'd build her a lake if that was what it took to convince her of returning to him. Unfortunately, it would have nothing to do with a lake.

The picnic blankets had already been spread out, and there was enough food and champagne to keep them going if they were stranded there for days. Caius took a blanket at the edge of the group, and Eliza joined him. The women really were giving her the cold shoulder. On some level it annoyed him, because she was by far the better person, but he knew that women could be prickly when a new woman was introduced to the group. They played power games. Men did too, but through different means. And these were not Eliza's kind of games.

"Do you wish to take one of the boats out on the lake?" he asked.

"That might be nice," she replied and they rose. Three small rowboats had been brought over for their use and Caius untied one of them and helped her step inside. The small boat swayed slightly as he stepped in and took his seat.

"I haven't rowed a boat since I was young, I think," he said, and moved them away from shore with strong, swift strokes.

"It is quite lovely. They have little boats like this in Hyde Park."

"I wasn't aware. I tend to stay away from Hyde Park. Too many people want to stop and chatter."

"Is that so awful?" she asked with a smile. Was that the first genuine smile he'd got from her?

"Yes," he confirmed. "If the conversation was modestly interesting it wouldn't be so bad. But gossip and fan-tailing, please spare me."

"Perhaps we have both become ill-suited to this company."

"I think so. Else we were only ever suited to each other."

Her smile slowly melted away and she stared down at her feet. "I can't just pick up where we left off. I simply can't."

"I am aware."

"Are you saying you can?"

He was quiet for a moment. "I'm not sure." This drew her attention back. From her perspective, he was perhaps contradicting himself. "I honestly don't know if I can settle. I am as uncomfortable and bored in their company," he said, nodding back at the shoreline they'd come from, "as you are. I have lived such a different life. Not one I particularly want to go back to, but I have found no balance here. You were my home here."

"Don't say that," she said, looking down again. "It isn't fair."

"No, it isn't. I know that as well as anyone, but it is nonetheless the truth. So if not with you, then I'm not sure I can stay."

"You were quite happy to divorce me not so long ago."

"I was driven by hurt and anger. And now I am not, but you still are."

"And now you want to rekindle and simply forget about everything. It is deeply unfair you placing ultimatums on me."

"It is not meant as an ultimatum. But I think you should know the truth. I cannot live here if you are here and living your own life, with another man."

"That directly contradicts what you said."

"I can only state the things I know and believe at the time. "

"And now you have changed your mind."

"I have simply understood my mind. Bickerley is yours, you can have it. The title, the money, everything."

"It is not mine. I never wanted to be Lady Warwick."

"You knew you eventually would be when you married me."

Silence descended between them. It was fair to say she was even more angry with him now than she'd been when she'd arrived here. It wasn't an ultimatum; it was simply the truth. It could be said it was manipulative, a gamble even, but it was still the truth. Then again, a gamble included some kind of bluff, and in his bones, he knew he wasn't bluffing.

Chapter 31:

WHEN SHE'D AGREED TO honesty between them, she might have agreed to more than she'd bargained for. Placing all this on her was unfair, but she also recognized in his eyes that he spoke the truth. Suddenly, she didn't want to be there, not that she'd really wanted to be there in the first place.

A complete awkwardness had descended between them. How was she supposed to take that? In a way it was sweet, in the way she'd imagined romance as a girl. In reality it wasn't sweet at all. His comfort and ability to settle in his own home was down to her. As gravely as she'd been injured, she was responsible for his happiness.

A part of her said that was simply part of being a wife, but that wife had been utterly discarded and dismissed, sent away unwanted.

Caius rowed in silence now and they made their way back.

"You ask too much," she said.

"I know," he replied.

And for a while there, she'd started to feel more comfortable in his company—likely because he was the only person there she knew.

With a silent, bitter chuckle, she recalled that she'd used to think getting divorced was making her life complicated, but it was nothing compared to not getting divorced.

What did he expect from her? That she relent simply because he was in an intolerable position. There was nothing to say he would settle even if she did. If she didn't know him, she would wonder if this was manipulative, but she knew it wasn't, she saw how awkward he was, how trying this all was for him.

But she wasn't responsible for him taking himself off to the end of the world and choosing the life of a soldier. She was innocent of that charge. More so than he was.

Please let me off this boat, she thought. At least he was taking her back, rather than keeping her out there on the middle of a lake, a captive. The shore was coming closer.

"I'm sorry," he said and she didn't know how to respond. There was a lot he was sorry for. There was a lot to be sorry for.

Words had dried up for her. There was nothing she wanted to talk about. As she watched, the shore came closer and eventually came the tug of the small boat gently grounding in the soft silt. Caius stepped past her and onto the shore. There were a few steps to the shore and his boots allowed it.

"Come," he said and reached for her hand. As she stood, he reached for her waist to lift her to shore. It felt both familiar and intimate, far more intimate than anything they'd done so far. Something perfectly normal for man and wife, except they weren't man and wife in reality. They were former, pretending not to be former in front of these people.

The pressure of having to safeguard that assumption descended on her again. Out of the frying pan and into the fire, she thought. A very different kind of discomfort, but right now, she preferred this lie to Caius' truths.

She returned to the blanket she'd sat on before, but Caius kindly gave her some space and was drawn into conversation with a couple of men talking some yards away.

A plate of late-season raspberries had been placed down and she nibbled a few, the sweet juice exploding on her tongue.

For a moment, she had to wonder if this was all worth it, all the discomfort of being here, but no, it was. Still, she didn't like it one bit.

"Beautiful day," a man said as he sat down and lay back on his elbows. Eliza barely remembered his name. Bertie, she believed. "We should enjoy days like this before winter sets in, shouldn't we?" He was speaking directly to her.

"Yes," she replied, and she had to agree. Days like this should be enjoyed, and maybe she should focus less on the unfairness of it all and more on being grateful for the beautiful location she found herself in. How long had it been since she'd sat down by a lake and simply enjoyed the sun? Truthfully, she couldn't remember. The business had taken most of her waking moments. Mostly because she enjoyed it and found it fulfilling, but she had been a little remiss in taking time to enjoy days like this. "One sometimes forgets the seasons living in the city."

"You live in London then? Not at Bickerley?"

Clearly he knew Caius well if he knew the name of his estate. She hadn't realized.

"No, I have commitments keeping me in the city at the moment." It didn't feel good stretching the truth, because the truth was that she had no plans on living elsewhere at all, even with Caius' offer that Bickerley was hers if he left.

"I suppose with winter coming up, London's the best place to be," the man continued. "My wife loathes London, so she waits until it is virtually unbearable before she joins me."

"You are a city creature then?" Eliza asked.

"I suppose I am. I do enjoy things a bit more lively. Caius used to be the same. Such a gregarious, happy person, but I have to admit, I don't recognize him anymore. He is simply not the easy-going man he was. You must find him much changed too."

For some reason the statement felt like a punch to her gut, because it was true. Even Caius had just said that he couldn't get back to what he was. His time away had changed him so radically, he couldn't settle anymore. And he held hopes that she could provide the means for him to do so. Rightly or wrongly.

"Are you alright, Lady Warwick?" he asked, suddenly looking concerned, which made her feel worse still. Something in all this pierced through a barrier she'd raised and she felt tears moisten her eyes. As much as she intellectually knew she wasn't responsible, how could she not feel so when he placed so much hope on her. She was the one not giving him what he needed.

"Excuse me," she said and quickly rose, feeling the need to escape, because she couldn't stop the emotions flowing. On quick feet, she rushed away from the group, needing a moment. A thicket of trees drew her and she hid in its shade, trying to get hold of the emotions that flowed unbid and unwanted.

"Are you alright?" Caius' voice said. He must have seen her and come after her.

With her fingers, she wiped her tears away. There was no point pretending she wasn't crying, because the evidence was undeniable. "I'm not sure..." she started.

"Did Bertie say something to you?" Caius asked, clearly concerned.

"No, nothing like that. It's just, this is all just a little overwhelming. I don't want to be here." With you, she wanted to say. This was just too hard, and whatever she did, she did something wrong. She couldn't be the wife he needed her to be. Forgiveness just wasn't in her right now. She couldn't just put all the hurt and broken trust to side and pick up where they'd left off. It just wasn't that simple.

Caius winced. "So, not Bertie, then. No matter what I do, I can't seem to stop making you cry."

"It's not..." she started again. Maybe he knew her well enough to read her, to recognize how she reacted to all this. What was there she could say to explain this, and her reticence? "You know, I'm not doing all this to reject you. I'm not even saying you don't deserve forgiveness, or maybe you don't. You are a victim in all this as much as I am, but I just can't... put everything behind me. I wish it was that easy."

With eyes down on the ground, he listened to what she said. "Maybe we have talked too much about this for one day."

That sounded imminently sensible to her, because she wasn't getting anywhere with it.

"We've had words on the topic," he continued, "and I think we are better leaving it for another day, so for now, instead we should remember why we are here. The children in the workhouses. Convincing Lord Sunderstone will have a marked impact on their lives. That is the reason you are here."

Absently she nodded, taking in his words. Yes, that was the reason they were there, and so much easier to focus on than the quagmire of emotions, hurts and injuries between them.

His eyes held such assurance when she looked up into them. How could he at the same time be the source of all her unease and also a comfort for her ambitions? It was almost as if he did marvelously as her friend, but miserably as her husband.

"Yes, you are right," she said, wiping away the last of the wetness from the corners on her eyes.

"And also, I have to say, that although I hate that I am responsible for your frequent burst of tears, I have to tell you that you look adorable when you cry."

Reaching out, she pinched his stomach, a familiar gesture she used to do when he teased her, and now it threatened a renewed wave of sadness, because those things where still there, along with all the hurt and badness underneath. It was what made this so hard to deal with, because she saw glimpses of her husband. But also, he had changed, as Bertie had noted. She saw that too.

Chapter 32:

CAIUS WAITED FOR ELIZA to arrive in the salon. Around him were as finely dressed people as he'd ever seen, and that included a number of people who hadn't been there earlier. Their party had swelled significantly with local gentry that Sunderstone had invited for the evening. It was labeled a party, but Caius expected there would be dancing involved, which made it far more than a party in his eyes.

Right now, however, he waited for Eliza to arrive. She's had her opportunity to put her proposal to Lord Sunderstone that afternoon. She'd talked and the man had listened carefully, but with little indication as to where his thoughts were. Not a man to make decisions lightly, so he would likely mull it over, and Eliza wouldn't have an answer until the man returned from France.

Once she'd made her case, she'd had the good sense not to push further. Eliza was good at reading people, had a mind for business, which was probably why she'd done so well.

After, she'd gone upstairs to rest. All in all, it had been a trying day for her and he hadn't really helped. Ahead of them was an evening of dancing and socializing, things he knew she wouldn't relish. Nor did he.

His musings were disturbed by her walking into the salon, wearing her nicest gown. Her eyes searched for him and stopped when she saw him. As opposed to what he feared, she didn't seek anyone else and came toward him.

"I hope you are well-rested," he said. "You look lovely."

"I am rather severely underdressed." Her eyes searched the ladies around her and she was more simply dressed than the colorful silks and satins. Rather than a simple country dance, some of these ladies were dressed for a royal ball. But as the season hadn't officially started yet, they were perhaps eager to display their new additions.

"Well, I don't think either of us have invested to any degree in our ball attire," he said wryly and received a smile from her.

"No, honestly, I haven't planned on any balls, or attended any since… you left."

"Then there is little disruption of my name appearing on your dance card." It might have been the wrong thing to say because she frowned and looked away. But he couldn't unsay it now. He seemed practically incapable of not saying things that reminded her of the ill things that had been.

"I think I may be too rusty to dance," she stated.

"Fine steps have not been a part of my life lately either, I must say. I think supper is being served," he said as he spied Sunderstone's butler entering the room. Eliza followed his gaze.

They walked with the rest of the gathered party into the dining room, where the table had been extended and many more placings had been laid out. There was a congenial chatter going on as everyone settled into their seats. Eliza sat next to him this time.

"Well, here you two are. You seem to be squirreled away somewhere together," said a woman whose name Caius couldn't remember. She leaned closer. "I wish my husband would look at me like yours looks at you," she said to Eliza.

Eliza's cheeks colored. Perhaps it looked that way to others.

"I suppose after so many years apart, you are like newlyweds again." The woman winked and laughed. It's been a pleasure to meet you. I do hope we'll see you both this winter. I will put you on my invitation list. We typically plan an evening around the second week in December."

"Oh, that is very kind," Eliza said, her cheeks still colored, because she couldn't really say anything else. It was kind of the woman to consider them, even if Eliza had no plans of them attending anything together. And it may not be that he stayed in England. Trying to imagine a long winter with nothing to do but to dodge invitations left him feeling queasy.

Fish was the main course and he enjoyed it. "The Chinese like fish a great deal, but their flavors are very different," he said after he'd finished. "We have more subtle seasoning."

"Do you like the Chinese dishes?"

"I do, but I'm not so proficient with their utensils. They have dexterity in their fingers that I cannot achieve."

"It must have been interesting experiencing such a different culture. I find it hard to imagine."

"It is a very established culture. They have their ways. On the whole, they are very friendly, but they are at the same time guarded. Family is important, and their relationship with the mystical. They're very superstitious. I don't entirely understand what their beliefs are, but everywhere you go, there's a shrine somewhere, in shops, residences, offices."

Around them, everyone was rising, so it was time to walk across to the ballroom, which was some distance from the dining room. Music was heard as they got closer, and footmen held trays of champagne in glasses, availing them to anyone who wanted one.

Taking two, he gave one to Eliza. She'd always liked champagne and sipped her glass. "I can't tell you how long it's been since I've had champagne," she said with a smile.

"I suppose these evenings do have some compensations."

"We must not be ungrateful," she chided. "Lord Sunderstone has been very kind to invite us. And hopefully he will conclude my proposal is beneficial."

"You might have to make an appointment with him on his return from the continent."

"Yes," she agreed. "But for right now, I think I've achieved as much as I can."

"Does that mean you wish to leave in the morning?"

She nodded. "Unless you want to stay."

"Not particularly. My objective here has been the same as yours." On one level that was true, but it also didn't comply fully with their edict for honesty. "And also to spend some time with you."

Color stained her cheeks again. It made her uncomfortable when he spoke about them and their relationship, and more often than not it ended in tears, which he didn't want. Time to change the subject. "I believe Bertie has the aim of a dance with you. Here he comes."

"Ah," Bertie said jovially as he joined them. "Splendid night, isn't it?"

"Yes," Eliza agreed. "This ballroom is quite magnificent."

"I do enjoy a ball. Caius was never that partial to dancing."

"Really? I recall a time when he was," Eliza said, and there had been a time when he'd come to every dance there was for a chance to dance with her. Every minute they could steal together, they would. Every dance had been something he would wait for with pounding heart.

"I was inspired," Caius said. "I only enjoy balls when Eliza attends." And that part was still true. He would attend every damn ball in the season if she were there. "Then again, if she were to go down a mine to dig coal, I would probably join her there too."

"Ah, so there is the trick. You have changed him completely."

Eliza looked lost for words for a moment. "He does have a way with words."

"Does he?" Bertie asked. "I never found him so. I think you bring about this change in him. But even so, I will endeavor to steal you away from him for the span of a dance."

"I would love to," she said with a smile.

An irrational spear of jealousy shot through Caius as Bertie led Eliza away to the dance floor, particularly as Bertie had managed to get a dance and he hadn't. But then he had been reticent to ask her.

As he watched, she went through the steps, looking as elegant dancing as he recalled. How many times had he stood in a ballroom watching Eliza dance, wishing it was him she danced with? Once they'd gotten engaged, he could claim more than two dances, but for some reason, once they'd married, they hadn't attended many balls. Maybe because he'd had the prize he'd sought.

Clearly she enjoyed dancing. He should have taken her to more dances. He should have kept people like William Garrick Castle away from her. How had he had such bad foresight? And then such lack of trust in her? Because he'd been devastated beyond reason, and reason had fled. Then he had fled.

The dance finally ended. "I'm sorry," he said when she returned to him, "for not taking you dancing more often once we married. In that light, I must insist on the next dance."

"Oh," she said and looked uncomfortable for a moment. She hadn't been uncomfortable as Bertie had led her on the dance floor, but he could see her nervousness now. Octavia appeared in his head, espousing what a good sign that was.

His heart beat like it had used to whenever he'd led her onto the dance floor, her gloved hand in his. How he wished it wasn't a barrier between them, but then again, the barrier between them had little to do with a glove.

The music flowed as did the steps, the currents of their movements. Nothing existed but her. Perhaps the unrecognized risk in all this was that he fell in love with her all over again, and would yet again be destroyed when it wasn't returned. Perhaps it was too late. There were no guarantees in either love or war. When it came down to it, all that could be was hope. And that was the position he now found himself in again.

Chapter 33:

THEY HAD BID FAREWELL to Lord Sunderstone the evening before, and he'd been merry with drink and dancing at the time, and had treated them like intimate friends. He'd also promised to see Eliza on his return to further discuss her interesting ideas. In her mind, she saw that as a hopeful development.

Only the servants were up and their carriage waited patiently for them outside as footmen carried their trunks down. All others were still in their beds, recovering from the evening before that had extended well beyond the time she and Caius had retreated to their rooms. Luckily their room was quite far away from the boisterous ballroom.

"Truthfully," Caius said as he sat down in the carriage after helping her get in, "I enjoyed last night more than I expected to. Attending a ball was the worst possible way I could imagine spending my time, but I did enjoy it."

"You always enjoyed balls."

"I enjoyed spending time with you, and that hasn't changed."

Biting her lip, she looked down into her lap. "Thank you for bringing me here. I do appreciate it, and am glad to hear it wasn't too onerous." Her emotions were still so harshly mixed. One moment she felt happy, the next she was in the pits of despair. How could she get a handle on her emotions? This wasn't like her. She was a steady creature, who focused on the practicalities. But then she'd never been indifferent to Caius, and that seemed a state she couldn't reach.

"Lord Sunderstone's parting words were encouraging," Caius said.

Outside the window, the parkland was moving by at the swift pace of horses eager with morning strength. Perhaps they were curious about where they were off to, or they expected to return to Bickerley where they likely belonged. "Not a bad day for travel." It was cool and crisp, the air clear. Too warm for a mist, but only just.

It was hard to find topics to discuss with him as they tended to veer straight to deep and painful sentiments, which left the weather and his travels. Every other topic seemed to tread on toes in one way or another, and she wished they could move away from that.

"How is your brother?" she asked.

"As of yet, he is unmarried. I believe Octavia is encouraging him to attend the season this year, but he keeps on sighing with discontent."

"If he wants a bride, he has to go out and find one. I'm assuming if there is an appropriate girl nearby, he would have married her already."

"Something seems to hold him back."

It had been the same six years back when they'd been together. Something was holding him back then too, and she suspected his heart was engaged elsewhere. Some woman had his heart and he couldn't get it back.

And there came a renewed wave of sadness, because in some ways, it reflected their own situation—unhappily in love. "Finding happiness isn't easy," she said, then wished she hadn't.

"It takes certain leaps of faith." It was a statement very much directed at her. She'd leapt and she'd suffered for it. How many times had she wished she'd never met Caius? William Castle Garrick was one thing, but it was Caius that had turned his back on her.

Not more of these emotions. "Mrs. Fisher, my housekeeper, says it should be a good raspberry season this year." For grasping for topics of conversation, that was an absurd one compared to heartfelt leaps of faith.

"You always liked raspberry jam."

How did he remember all these things, especially after he'd spent so much effort trying to forget her, according to his own admission.

"I left because the worst thing I could imagine happened," he said, the statement taking her by surprise. They were having two different conversations vying for attention. Admittedly, her conversation was about the raspberry season, his was the deepest feelings in his heart.

There was nothing she could say. Should she accuse him yet again of not having faith in her and assuming that stupid man's statement was true? What was the point?

"Maybe I feared the power you had over me. Because one careless act would utterly destroy me."

"But there was no careless act."

"I believed there had been, perhaps I'd been waiting for the fear to eventuate."

This was something new, something she hadn't heard before.

"I feared being so vulnerable, and it felt as if the minute I was, I was punished for it. And yes, maybe I refused to look too closely. I just fled, because I'd already taken the blow. In some sense, I don't think it would have mattered if it was true or not. The blow was real, and I wasn't strong enough to withstand it."

Eliza blinked. She didn't know what to say, how to react to this.

"I don't think I was ready to be your husband in every way it entailed. Don't get me wrong, I loved being your husband in terms of being in love and having a grand time, attending parties and the honeymoon—but everything else, the harder things, the blows. I don't think I had the maturity and wisdom to deal with them. I was too young. So when the first blow came, and it was a powerful one, I didn't know how to deal with it. Until then, the only things I worried about were losing poker games and incurring my father's displeasure."

Silence descended within the carriage. Maybe this accusation stretched to her too. She'd been so absorbed with being victimized that she couldn't see beyond the wrong that had been done to her.

And to be fair, her distance now wasn't because of offense that she'd been wronged, but because she couldn't trust enough to put her heart on the line. "I think it could be said, we were both too young to deal with the situation with maturity."

"And we destroyed our marriage because of it." His words were harsher than hers, but yes, they had. “And now," he said slowly and she held her breath, because she wasn't sure she wanted to hear what he was about to say. "And now I wish to court you."

"What?"

"I wish to go to every stupid ball in London and put my name on your dance card."

"You hate balls."

"I never hated balls when I was courting you."

How was it he always managed to leave her stumped for words? More importantly, how did she feel about this? It did circumvent the strife she felt at just picking up where they'd left off. That felt wrong and she couldn't just plow through that barrier, but courting? It had some possibilities. In her mind, she could almost imagine it.

"Perhaps," she started, "as neither of us, as grown adults, particularly like balls or society parties, we could find another way."

"I suppose we don't exactly need the chaperoning system of the society drawing rooms. Saying that, courting you throughout the season would provide the perfect excuse for dragging my brother through said ballrooms of London. What kind of a brother would I be if I didn't force him around town until he found someone to his liking, or rather someone who could tolerate him."

Eliza chuckled. "Then perhaps we simply need to endure. And that is a little ungenerous. Your brother is perfectly tolerable, if a little prickly at times. I am sure the perfect girl is out there somewhere." And if Julius couldn't find a single person after a season, maybe there was no hope for him if some lost love really had his heart so completely. She hoped not. That would be sad and awful. Maybe a fate that awaited all of them if they didn't try a little. It was worth trying, wasn't it?

A lightness filled her, because he was giving her time. He was giving her a means of adjusting, one step at a time. Or one cotillion at a time. They could get to know each other again, and in a way that did always delve into their deepest injuries every time they spoke to each other.

Never would she have expected she'd be attending the season again. But something about this was amusing, and one thing they'd always done well together was having a grand time. And frankly, a day ago she'd have balked at the idea. Now, a certain excitement was growing in her.

Something was melting away inside her. Maybe her wounds had been exorcised to the point where there was nothing left there. It had been a painful and trying exercise, she had to admit, one they'd both have to go through.

The very idea of putting the past behind her was exciting, but she was jumping to conclusions. This was to be a slow process, one dance at a time, one ball at a time, and maybe the love that had been there would flourish again, as would their enjoyment of being in each other's company.

Hope flared in her heart and it had a painful tinge, but the pleasure of it far outweighed the pain. Maybe she did dare let him closer once again.

There was a lightness about him too, a smile lingered on his lips. Of course the season was at least a month and a half away. Suddenly that seemed like a really long time.

Chapter 34:

THEY'D STOPPED AT AN inn and had eaten roast lamb. Unpleasant weather had rolled in for the last part of their journey, but it didn't diminish his mood, because Eliza smiled and even laughed. She was still guarded, but the scowl was gone, and that could only be a good thing.

And they had a plan, a means of finding their way back to each other. Eliza had been curious about it, so come hail or high water, he would be accepting an invitation to every ball in the city this winter.

In the meantime, he might write to her. What were a courting couple without love letters? Octavia would have to help him. Fine sentiments on paper were well out of his realm of experience. And he didn't even wish to recall his clumsy attempts as a young man, where he'd rather have died than have shown them to Octavia, and they were worse off for it.

The narrow streets of Lambeth were slow to get through, but they arrived at Eliza's house. It was raining heavily and the driver handed down an umbrella as he got out and walked her the few steps to the door.

Water flowed off the sides of the umbrella. Proper autumn rain.

At the door, Eliza stopped and turned to him. "Thank you again for taking me. It was an interesting excursion and hopefully the start of a business relationship that will go on for some time."

"I think we also discussed some things that needed to be said."

"Yes, I suppose."

"And now starts our official courtship. And what courtship doesn't start with a stolen kiss?"

Her mouth open in surprise and it was the opportunity he took, claiming her lips and kissing her like he'd wanted to so many times. The sweetness of it suffused his mind. Her lips soft, but reticent. There wasn't rejection there, but she wasn't abandoning herself to it completely. It was nice. The first of many, he hoped.

Breaking the kiss, he walked back to the carriage so she didn't have a chance to rebuke him. As she stood on her doorstep, her fingers pressed to her lips and he waited for her to slip inside. And then he sighed, still feeling the ghost of the kiss, the taste of her. It had been such a long time since there had been a kiss between them. In the rush at the end of their relationship, such animosity, he didn't actually remember when the last kiss had been. Likely some quick kiss as she'd walked in or out of a room, that neither of them had expected to be the last one. Well, now it wasn't the last and hopefully this one wouldn't be either.

"Let's get off home, Joseph," he said to the driver and they drove off. It felt wrong leaving her behind, but that was what they'd agreed. In the morning, he'd continue onto Denham. It was time to take Octavia back and he also needed to twist Julius' arm into attending the season. It would take some time to achieve, but they had time. Too much for his liking, but it was what it was.

*

"Brother," Caius said as he arrived at Denham Hall. Octavia walked in beside him and went to her typical seat in the salon.

"It's so nice to be home. London is utterly mad," she stated. "And I think we all need to spend the winter there."

"What, no!" Julius said.

Caius had discussed the plan for the season with Octavia during the carriage ride and they were in agreement. Julius was to spend the season in London, attending every ball with his siblings.

"Caius needs to make an effort wooing his wife, and you need to support him," Octavia said.

"What, no!"

"You cannot hide away in the country all your life. Caius needs your help."

"He doesn't need me to hold his hand."

"As you are unmarried, we need the excuse. Caius needs a chance to charm Eliza."

"You're unmarried too," Julius accused.

"Yes, but it will look more strange me being chaperoned by my brother. We are better off all going. It will be fun. It's been years since we've spent a winter in London," Octavia countered.

"No, it won't. It will be awful."

"Well, you're coming all the same," Octavia said with her arms crossed, and they both knew she wouldn't be changing her mind when she took this stance and would pester until every ounce of resistance was defeated.

"Fine," Julius said ahead of one of Octavia's onslaughts.

"I wonder if Cecilia Blackwell will be there."

"That awful girl. I'm not surprised she's still unmarried."

"Yes, well, she is too choosy for her own good. There isn't a man in the country she hasn't turned down already. I guess it's your turn."

"Ugh, never," Julius replied.

"Never what?" Father said, walking into the salon, dressed to go out, which he rarely did.

"Never deal with designing women," Julius said.

"We are all spending the season in London," Octavia said brightly.

"Oh thank heaven. Months of peace without you all," Father said tartly. "Well, have fun. When do you leave?"

"Not for another month at least."

"Right," Father said. "I'm going to see Mr. Chateron about that stallion of his. We should come to some kind of agreement on the stud fees for spring."

"Oh, I'll come," Julius said, partially to get away from Octavia's planning for their future.

Throughout his life, Caius had never developed the interest in horses that his father and brother shared. He appreciated his horses, of course, but beyond getting him where he wanted to go and doing so without biting, he couldn't care less about their pedigree or breeding benefits.

Julius followed his father out and Octavia retreated to her room to freshen up after the journey. It still rained outside.

It still felt strange being back here. They all tended to revert to their younger selves when they were together, and there was something nostalgic about it. Now he had to wait out some weeks here before the season started. In that time, the days would grow colder, the bad weather becoming more frequent. At times when he'd been gone, he'd missed this time of the year, after the harvest when everything slowed down. The fields were burned and the yard was bedded down for the winter.

At the window, he saw the apple tree he used to climb on a regular basis. In his time away, he seemed to have grown distant from the person he'd used to be, the husband he'd been, and even the child that had grown up here.

How he wished Eliza was here, and that they could talk the way they'd used to. Almost like a ghost, he could see her walking around the salon, chattering like she'd used to about whatever she'd learned from whoever had come calling to the house. Would they get there again? There was hope, and right now he couldn't bring himself to consider the alternative.

*

"We really should have brought father with us," Octavia said as they walked into the family's Belgravia townhouse.

Excitement at seeing Eliza was coursing through Caius' veins. It felt like it'd been months, when it'd only been one month. He'd received one letter from her in that time, and he'd written two. Writing sentiments wasn't his strength, so they'd been short and had mainly described what he'd been up to, and how his siblings were looking forward to seeing her during the season.

Luckily, Octavia had taken care of all invitations and responses, which was a surprisingly time-consuming activity.

"He wouldn't come even if Denham burned to the ground." Julius said tartly.

The house was nicely warm as they'd given the staff notice of their arrival, and truthfully, it was nice, because Denham was impossible to heat during the cold months. At the very worst weather, some rooms even had ice on the windows, and that was on the inside of the panes. This was much more comfortable.

"Now I think we should call on Sophia Worthingham tomorrow," Octavia said.

"Calling is where I draw the line," Julius said flatly.

"How are you supposed to get to know these women if you don't call on them?"

"You're enjoying this much too much," Julius accused. "I will only be pushed so far."

Octavia rolled her eyes and Caius left them to squabble. Julius' accusation was true. Octavia was enjoying every moment torturing her brother, but he'd agreed to come, which meant that on some level, he was seeking a wife. Granted his prospects would be looked on much more favorably if he'd received his title, but that could be decades away and Julius would be of risk of getting set in his ways at some point.

Because Julius could be just as stubborn as their father, he wouldn't have come if there was nothing in him that felt he needed to be here. Julius wanted a wife—not that he wouldn't complain the entire way.

"I'm going for a walk," Caius said, feeling the need to stretch his legs after the long journey. The carriage had been cramped with the three of them.

The air was brisk outside, but not sweet like the air at Denham. But the excitement of the city was around him and he was on his way to his club to see if there was anything new to try on their whiskey shelf.

His heart wanted to walk south, but he wasn't going to push seeing her. There was a certain sweetness in anticipation. The next time he saw her would be at a ball in a few days' time and she would be dressed in a new gown. At least he hoped so. He'd set up an account under his name at one of the celebrated seamstresses in the city and urged Eliza to order whatever she required.

It could be that she still refused his assistance in all things, but he hoped not. He also recognized that Eliza could probably afford to buy her own gowns, but it wouldn't be something she would do if he wasn't insisting on courting her at every ball in town.

It was a mad idea, but it had seemed like a brilliant compromise at the time. And he would probably hate having to attend balls, but he was so excited to see her.

"Afternoon, Lord Warwick," the attendant at the door said as he reached his club. "We are pleased you could join us today." The man took his hat and coat.

"Thank you, Turner. Thought I would sample some of Mr. Waincoat's new purchases."

"I believe he has tracked down some nice bottles. Scoured the country."

"Excellent," Caius said and walked into the warm, comfortable surrounds of his club. His ease this time was much stronger than the last time he'd been here, which must have been after one of his tear-inducing interactions with Eliza. Hopefully those were at an end. There had been enough of her tears. Now he wanted joy and laugher, and he'd do just about anything he could to make her laugh.

Men greeted him, getting more used to seeing him here now. He wasn't such an oddity anymore, a remarked stranger in their midst.

"Ah, Lord Warwick," Mr. Waincoat said. "I believe I have something that will delight you."

"Wonderful," Caius said. "That warms my heart on a cold and dreary day like this."

Taking the bottle down, the man poured him a measure into a glass, and Caius took a sip and savored it. Both sweet, smooth and bitter, all at once. "That is a lovely find."

"I think so," the man said and nodded as Caius grabbed a copy of the paper and found his seat in the sparsely attended parlor.

Chapter 35:

ELIZA TRIED NOT TO MOVE as sharp pins surrounded her. Looking down, she saw the rich, light blue material that shimmered with light.

"It's a stunning dress," Teresa said, sitting in a velvet-covered chair at a dressmaker Eliza hadn't used before.

"Apparently I am not living up to the expectations of Lady Warwick," Eliza said, considering herself in the mirror. It was a gorgeous gown. She didn't dare think how expensive it was. Caius insisted on her putting it on the Warwick account. She had mixed feelings about doing so, but also recognized she wouldn't be getting this dress if it wasn't for him.

In the last few weeks, she'd gone back and forth about this idea of attending balls. At times, she was beside herself with excitement. Other times, it seemed a silly and stupid idea. But one thing she had learned was that she'd missed him. It was a surprise, but it was true nonetheless. At times, she'd wanted to point out something to him, but he wasn't there—wasn't even in London.

"Are you sure this is a good idea?" Teresa asked. "Is this what you want?"

"Going to balls? No, I can't say that it is."

"Then why are you doing it?"

It took her a while to answer, while the French seamstress pinned more needles around her skirt. "I suppose it is an avenue to..."

"Rekindle?"

"Get to know each other again. We're both different people now. Do you think I'm being silly?" Eliza asked, looking back at Teresa through the mirror. A voice in her head was accusing her of being weak and folding—that her fortitude had stood for nothing.

Teresa shifted and crossed her arms. "I suppose it's something that he is willing to try. And he doesn't hit you."

"No, of course not," Eliza said with an immediate frown. Whenever Teresa talked about her husband, it sounded like a horrific marriage.

"I take it you believe he's changed for the better," Teresa continued. "Personally I would never put trust in any man."

"I don't want to be the kind of person who can't put trust in a man, and I don't think you should be either. There are good men in the world."

Teresa sniffed. "Maybe if I had a man who was willing enough to attend every ponsy ball in the city, I might consider it."

"Why don't you come with me?"

"To a toff ball? I'd rather poke my eyes out. I'd stick out like a sore thumb."

"No, you wouldn't. Quite a few people know who you are. You've met just about every charity in the country." When they'd prepared for Eliza's divorce, they had quite firmly placed Teresa as the head of the company. "You should come."

"No, I couldn't imagine anything more uncomfortable. I'm not made for ball gowns."

"Going alone isn't ideal as I'm technically not arriving with my husband. It will definitely get the gossips going—unless I am introducing someone."

"Well, it won't be me. Why don't you take that Jane Brightly girl?"

"Who?" Eliza searched her mind, but the name didn't spark any recognition.

"That orphan girl who applied to work as an illustrator. She's from a good family."

"She did? I don't recall."

"I did mention it, or rather shouted it down to you in your pit of despair."

"Right. Sorry, I don't recall."

"Yes, well, she's found herself in unfortunate circumstances and is currently without means of supporting herself and has no family to speak of. She'll have the right pedigree, and will probably hold her teacup right."

"There aren't typically teacups at balls."

"See, there. I don't know those kinds of things."

"So this Jane Brightly applied to be an illustrator? What did you say?"

"I said I'd see if we have any such work available, and that we do have illustrators we use already. I haven't sent any work her way yet. I thought I'd give her a try when the opportunity arose."

Eliza frowned, feeling sorry for the girl, remembering what it was like arriving in London with nothing but her trunk. It was terrifying. "Where is she?"

"Brighton, I believe. She's staying in some boarding house."

"Poor thing."

"Well, I take it she could most definitely not afford being debuted at the society balls."

"True," Eliza said, looking at herself in the mirror. This girl might not have the appropriate wardrobe, but that could be fixed. Caius wouldn't even notice if she added three additional dresses to the account. "I could enact her debut. It would be a purpose for me being there. Brighton, did you say?"

Teresa nodded. "I'm sure she'll come if we asked her to."

"It would be the opportunity of a lifetime for her, being debuted during the season." It would give this whole venture a real purpose, other than her and Caius... She didn't even know what to call it. Nerves clenched in her stomach. "Well, we'd better get her up here quick smart if we're to get some dresses made for her."

"You sure you want to do this? We have no idea what you're committing to. She could be ugly as sin and painfully shy."

"Shush. I'm sure she is perfectly lovely. And everyone deserves a chance."

"Well, that will officially make more strays that we can accommodate in the house."

Biting her lips together, Eliza considered the options. Taking on a debutant usually involved housing them, not that Lambeth was a particularly good neighborhood in terms of making an impression. And placing her in a lodging house was even worse. "I suppose I could ask Octavia to house her."

"That might scare her off for good."

"Octavia would treat her kindly."

"Like she did you for years on end?"

Teresa was slower to forgive the family on how Eliza had been treated than Eliza herself. Perhaps that was understandable. Emotions did color things. She certainly would never understand if Teresa decided to forgive her brute of a husband, but women were capable of going back to horrid, violent men.

"Well, let's propose it and see if she's interested," Eliza said. "She might think it's odd. Maybe I should write to her." And somehow explain that she was searching for a companion and would use a debut as an excuse. If she received such a letter herself, she might think twice about accepting, but if this girl's circumstances were as dire as Teresa suggested, she would jump at the chance. And Eliza felt obliged to consider her for work as an illustrator either way. Maybe they just had to think of some project that would need illustration.

*

Standing at Victoria station with Teresa, Eliza considered the solitary young ladies coming off the train from Brighton. There weren't too many. It shouldn't be overly hard to find her, she hoped.

Pairs came and then a solitary girl looking lost. She was short and blond, and wore a hat, which Eliza suspected had been her school hat. It wasn't technically appropriate, but she could understand the girl using it if she had nothing else.

"Gad, she looks like a little pixie," Teresa said and pulled her arm away from Eliza's. "Jane?" she called to the girl, who looked over and smiled. Her eyes were bright and clearly intelligent. This was a good choice, Eliza knew. She liked the girl already.

"Hello," the girl said as she came over. "I wasn't entirely sure if your letter was serious, but how could I not come and see. My name is Jane Brightly. You must be Teresa and Eliza." Her voice was clear and strong. There was a strong will there, Eliza knew, strength that had seen her through her trials and tribulations.

"Yes, it is a bit of a madcap idea, so it's understandable you're sceptical, but we felt this was something that could help both of us. My husband's family has kindly agreed to house you throughout this. And after, we can talk about illustration work."

"Right," Jane said. "Thank you so much. I can't stress enough what a delight this is."

"I hope you like balls," Teresa said with a note of terseness.

"I haven't had the opportunity to attend many."

"Then this is your chance. I've made an appointment with a seamstress for you tomorrow," Eliza said.

The girl's mouth opened in shock. "I couldn't possibly… I mean to say my means are rather limited."

"My husband is paying," Eliza said with a dismissive wave of her hand. And not that long ago, she'd hated accepting her husband's charity, but had had no choice. It was a point of pride, and just because one had no means didn't mean feeling terrible accepting charity. "And I told him you would do some illustrations for him in return." It was a lie, but it made Jane brighten. Now she had to recall this to inform Caius when she saw him. "It will all be lovely, you'll see."

And hopefully Octavia wouldn't be unkind due to Jane's reduced circumstances. Octavia wasn't an unkind person, except to anyone who hurt her brothers. A warning in that regard was likely entirely unnecessary.

Chapter 36:

"WHO IS THAT GIRL?" Julius asked as he entered the salon.

"Jane," Octavia said, but didn't elaborate further. "I expect you to be nice to her."

"When am I not nice?"

"Most of the time."

"Why is she living in our house?" he said in a loud whisper.

"Because Eliza asked us to house her."

"So we're housing every scamp in the city now? We simply house whomever she asks us to? We don't know anything about her. She could rob us blind during the night."

"Yes, because we are trying to make a good impression on her."

"That girl?"

"No, Eliza. Although that girl seems cordial enough. Eliza is debuting her."

"Is Eliza sure she is old enough?" Julius said, taking a seat next to Caius, who had so far not participated in this conversation, mostly because time was drawing near and his desire to see Eliza was so strong it was trying his patience.

"Yes, she is old enough. And Eliza's house isn't big enough to house her. The girl's prospects are abysmal."

"Then it is unlikely that someone will marry her," Julius said with a snort.

"I don't know. I think she has a quality men will find irresistible. She has a certain ethereal quality. I think those of a more romantic disposition will find her intriguing."

Julius snorted.

"A solid ledger doesn't always make for a good marriage," Caius finally said.

"Romantic poppycock."

"Romance certainly has gripped your soul, hasn't it, Julius?" Octavia challenged.

"I know that those with wealth and connections beyond others have their pick," Julius said bitterly. It seemed Eliza might be right and that Julius had some personal experience in that regard, but he'd never shared why. There was something in his past that had made him withdraw, and they'd never understood why.

"Pick of what, though?" Octavia challenged. "Pick of those greedy enough to want that wealth?"

The conversation was interrupted by Jane walking into the room. Caius had been introduced, but as he wasn't staying there, he hadn't had a chance to say more than hello. Octavia was the one dealing with her. Where Eliza had found her, Caius had no idea, but she knew all sorts of people he didn't through her work with charities.

She wore a shimmery, light blue dress and it did make her look ethereal. The girl was barely over five foot and was quite enchanting when she smiled. Her nerves were clear. "Hello," she said. "I hope I haven't kept you waiting."

"It was worth the wait," Octavia said and rose. "I believe the carriage is ready. It will be a bit of a squeeze the four of us."

"There are only so many ball gowns one can fit in a carriage," Julius said.

"Shush," Octavia directed. "Help Jane if she needs it." Octavia smiled at the girl. "Shall we?"

The carriage ride wasn't more than five minutes, and the girl was almost overly polite, saying thank you every time Julius helped her, which he looked exceedingly exasperated with.

Lanterns led the way up the stairs and footmen were standing by to receive coats and accoutrements. Music lingered in the air and the windows were brightly lit. Beside him, he heard the girl draw in a shaky breath. She smiled tentatively when Caius looked over. They were both nervous and both waiting for Eliza to arrive.

Truthfully, he knew so little about the girl, it was hard to make conversation, and this wasn't the time or the place to divulge life stories. "An interesting night awaits."

"I hope so," she said and lifted the gown as she took the last step into the house. It was a spectacular gown. And a few men noted her as she walked in. Perhaps Octavia was right in that regard.

His eyes searched for Eliza, ignoring the people who were trying to draw his attention. He would speak to them eventually, but right now, he had a priority. She wasn't to be found and for a moment, he worried that she'd changed her mind. How quickly his emotions turned to despair. These emotions were torturing him. One moment elated and then the pits of despair. This had to take a toll on his heart, but he couldn't turn away from this, everything he needed was in this direction, and it walked through the door right then, wearing a rose-colored gown. She looked stunning.

She smiled for a moment as she walked toward him and for an instance he forgot where he was. She'd come. That meant something. It meant that her promise to give this a try hadn't diminished in their time apart. It had been hard to give her the space she needed, to not rush over there and ensure her opinion of him wasn't slipping at any point. It was important not to be overbearing, even as his instinct told him to hold on tighter.

"Caius," she said as she came to him.

"Eliza. You look stunning."

"Thank you. It's a new gown."

"I like it." It did look sufficiently regal for the location. No one would fault this gown for being subpar for a society ball.

"And Jane, you look lovely."

The girl blushed. "I'm so excited, I'm beside myself." The girl said, taking a deep breath, but the tight stays of the gown made it hard. "There are so many people."

It was crowded. It seemed everyone in London was here. Caius saw faces he knew and faces he couldn't put names to. Wasn't particularly bothered to, because he wasn't there for them.

"Have you got a dance card?" Eliza asked.

"No, not yet," Jane said, looking around as if to gain some understanding of how that was done.

"We'll go get ours together. Goodbye, Caius," Eliza said and smiled as she took Jane's arm and wandered off. It signified that she was fully intending on making him woo her. Challenge placed and challenge accepted.

As he watched, Eliza and Jane retrieved their dance cards and then continued with Jane's introductions. It'd been quite a while since Eliza had been seen in this society as well, but that wasn't strictly unusual with married women.

Caius allowed himself to be drawn into conversation by some of the men who'd tried to draw his attention. Horses, investments, questions about his time in the Far East. It appeared he was now an expert on politics, trade and cultural conventions of the whole of the Far East.

As soon as the first dance started, he excused himself and made his way to where Eliza was introducing Jane to Lord Torpington and his nondescript son. A young man who looked bored out of his wits. Again Caius recognized that people in their society married too young. Even if they make decisions about who to marry, they weren't equipped to deal with it. Or perhaps that was by design. It was easier to guide a youngster into accepting a beneficial marriage, while someone wiser might prioritize happiness over family benefit.

Because at his age, he would laugh at his father for trying to shift his attention from where it wanted to be. Julius saw things differently. The future of the family name and the title still weighed on him, as had been ground into him from the time he was old enough to listen. Perhaps it was that weight that kept him from finding a woman he could consider as a wife.

"I will be disappointed if you haven't reserved the first dance for me," he said softly in Eliza's ear. A smile spread across her lips and she looked at him.

"Luckily for you, my attention has been exclusively on filling Jane's dance card."

"Good, because although I would like to think of myself as a reasonable man, when it comes to your dance card, I suffer from curious bouts of irrationality."

"We're not back to irrationality, are we?" she said, turning to him.

"I'm trying very hard not to, so if you must dance with other men, make them as old and unattractive as possible. Ideally lame."

A chuckle escaped her and he loved that he could make her laugh. Not long ago, nothing he said gave her the least bit of amusement. "I suppose you'd better ask me then."

"Lady Warwick, Eliza, it would give me the greatest honor if you would give me your first dance. I suppose every dance would be too much to ask for."

"Much too much," she chided. "But yes, I will give you my first dance."

Jane was being claimed by her first dancing partner, so Caius had Eliza all to himself for the first time in weeks. Not perhaps as much to himself as he wanted, but there was a deep excitement leading her onto the dance floor.

Once taking their spot, his hand sought her waist and he felt as if all was right again. "I've missed you," he confessed and she blushed. "So many times, I wanted to come speak to you."

"Then why didn't you?"

"Perhaps you needed a chance to miss me too? Obviously I want to ask you if you did."

"Do you?"

The steps started, and Caius realized he had no idea what dance they were doing and was hoping that out of the deep recesses of his mind, he'd remember the steps. "Did I tell you I haven't danced in years?"

"That makes both of us."

They were going through the steps, at points that half-beat behind everyone else. "I don't think we're going to win any prizes. A lifelong ambition dashed," he said sarcastically. "I do remember our wedding however." It was a day where he'd been as happy as he'd ever been.

A slight sadness entered her eyes and he wished he hadn't said anything. And he wished he didn't feel on tenterhooks with every emotion fleeting through her eyes, but this all felt so tentative. It was tentative. She was giving them a chance, and he was grateful. As was he grateful for how lovely she felt in his arms.

Octavia passed by and she was dancing with a young man she didn't look overly enthusiastic about. Meanwhile Jane was laughing not much further away, clearly delighted by the evening, the experience and the company. No, Octavia was right. Some young buck would be enchanted by her.

Julian was nowhere in sight, probably sulking in the cards room. Right now, however, Caius didn't care about anything other than his wife. Unless there were torn limbs and bleeding involved, they would all simply have to take care of themselves.

"Are you enjoying the ball?" he asked, as she returned to him after the steps took her away.

"I am actually."

The dance was ending and they drifted off. Jane was being approached by whoever had claimed her second dance. "I think your charge is a success."

"I think her circumstances will make things difficult for her, but you never know. She might meet the right man who will look past her diminutive means."

"Some are wise enough to not consider means in the first instance. Marriage is a lifelong commitment, and we both know that it can be miserable if you make a hash of it."

"Yes," she said, letting him lead her toward where the drinks were being served. French champagne was offered and they accepted two glasses.

"I am still thinking of Paris," he said after taking a sip.

"One step at a time," she said with a smile. "You are being awfully forward in this courting. I wouldn't skip the wooing part for a minute. I find I'm enjoying it immensely."

"Then I am doing something right." Something about what she said put him at ease, because she seemed primarily interested in enjoying his company.

"Although strictly speaking, if we were courting, it would be unseemly to spend every moment of the ball together."

"I am fully open to being unseemly," he replied with a smile.

"You're incorrigible," she replied with a nudge. As she put down her drink, she pulled out her fan and fanned herself. The dancing was starting to heat the room and the first dance had been vigorous.

"Even more scandalously, I might try to tempt you into a turn in the fresh air. I believe there is a veranda facing the garden. Shall we?"

She considered him for a moment, placing the top of the fan to her nose. "Some fresh air might be bracing," she admitted, "provided my beau behaves himself." Her hand snaked around his elbow.

"I might fear the sting of a slap if I don't." It wasn't something he feared, but he did enjoy the teasing banter they'd shifted toward. From where they'd come from, it was a vast improvement.

Chapter 37:

THE COOL AIR STROKED the skin of her arms and face as she walked outside and took a deep breath. The heat inside was trying and it felt like there was so much on the line today. Jane's acceptance into this society, which wasn't assured, although she seemed to be garnering some admirers. They would all discover that she wasn't a new heiress in their midst, but the impoverished girl from an unfortunate but genteel family.

And Caius. It felt... familiar, exciting, nerve-wracking, chaotic being the object of his attention again. It lulled her and drew her in. He'd been her sun for a while and she was in that position again. He radiated his warmth, fun and hope, and she once again basked in his attention.

Taking a sip of her champagne, she let the bubbles linger in her mouth as she thought about how this night was faring. It was so all-encompassing when her and Caius were in harmony. Everything was so bright, it outshone everything else.

"It's not too cold?" he asked.

"No," she replied. Other people lingered around them, staying by themselves at various parts of the veranda. The stars shone above them and the air had the distinct freshness of early winter. The warmth would seep away, and there would be frost in the morning. The garden below was dark as water, and to the side was what looked like a greenhouse. She could imagine who owned it would quite happily potter inside it throughout long winter days.

"So is there any chance I could woo you in Paris as well?" he asked, a smile lingering on his lips.

"You do have an urge to see Paris, it seems?"

"I think you would enjoy it. I hear spring is unsurpassed."

Before her, she could see them doing such things together, enjoying being together, exploring the world around them. It was such a departure from where her life had been. Her business had been everything she'd thought about and accepting Caius into her life meant broadening that perspective, and he might want to jaunt off to Paris for no particular reason. Accepting him meant accepting that they would spend time together.

Then again, in their urgency to prepare for his impact on her life, she and Teresa had already set up Teresa as the future of the company in the eyes of everyone they dealt with. It turned out not to be necessary, but it was done, so in many ways she could draw other things into her life, like travel and excursions.

"You are so very sure," she said.

"About going to Paris?"

"About what you want."

"Yes. I am sure."

How she wished she felt it. It wasn't that she doubted his sincerity, or even his ability to be a good husband. He would give as much as she would accept. It wasn't that she was afraid—it was more than her battered heart hurt being filled up again. These emotions between them were so very big, and the scars took some time to stretch.

"I do love you," she could hear herself saying, not quite sure why. It was the truth. She'd never stopped, and perhaps that was the reason she'd been so cautious.

Caius was quiet for a moment, his face in darkness. "I never stopped loving you, although there were times I would have cut it out if I could have. While there are many things I regret, I don't regret being here with you right now."

A blush stained her cheeks and her heart ached, another scar being stretched. The worst of them had perhaps been dealt with, but the sweetness made up for the pain.

With his hand, he reached for her, drawing her into a kiss. Warm lips met hers, the familiar taste of him compelling, smooth and exciting. It deepened and they melted together. Her insides awoke and a quickening of desire flared, wanting to feel every part of him to her. His tongue stroked hers as he explored her mouth, slowly and gently.

A slow exhale escaped her lips as the kiss broke. A deep, heady energy flowed down into her very bones. Her body recognized the man she'd loved, still loved. If he kissed her like that, she would agree to just about anything, but they were seen. In darkness, but seen by the others lingering in the cool air of the veranda.

Still, she couldn't pull away from him, her hands lingered on his stomach, feeling the material of his shirt and his firm body underneath.

"One dance and I'm putty in your hands," she said, her voice a little shaky. "I really am disturbingly easy to woo.

My mother would be ashamed of me if she found me kissing the first man I danced with."

"Ah, I see what you mean, but rest assured that this man is more than grateful. Yes, I suppose you need to be careful, because I have now come to expect a kiss after every dance."

"Have you now? That is awfully presumptuous."

"Some would say hopeful."

Hopeful might not be the right word. She didn't know what was because her lips ached for another kiss, another taste of him. The fire lit in her belly. Desire. It had been so long since she'd felt it, because it had been twinned with longing, which she'd strictly forbidden herself from feeling. But she longed for him, for his touch, his lips, his heart.

Without letting her thoughts or fears intrude, she stepped closer and claimed another kiss. Sweet and soft, deepening with every passing moment. Energy flowed between them, coursing through every part of her body. She wanted more. Her lungs burned for air, but she wanted the kiss more. Finally she had to break it, her breath shaky as she tried to breathe again.

"Now it is definitely dangerous to steal a kiss from the first man you dance with. It might..."

"It might what?"

"Test his restraints. And it might prime him to be tortured by your mere presence for the rest of the night. Every touch, scent and look would be sheer agony."

Another kiss came crashing down on her lips, harsh this time, filled with desire. It urged deeper into her mouth, claiming more than exploring. His lips moving on hers, his tongue reaching deeper, stroking along hers. His arms held her tight and she felt every part of him, caught in sheer desire. A moan reverberated through her mouth and down into her body.

She groaned as the kiss broke, her body on fire. Deep in her belly, she ached for him, for his touch, for him coming to her in a way a husband did. She wanted the pleasure he could give her; she burned for it.

"I am utterly failing at this courting adventure," she stated. "I shamelessly want you at a society ball where every tattling matron in the country is roaming not far away. I only managed one dance. I am deeply disappointed with myself."

The smile was impossible to stop as he reached up and tucked a wisp of hair behind her ear. Was her hair coming undone too?

"I have to admit such kisses do stop men from seeing reason. Come," he said.

"Come where?"

"Into the darkness, where a young woman should absolutely not go with the first man she dances with." His hand reached for hers, softly threading his fingers between hers. And she wanted the touch, she wanted their coming together in every profound way possible. Her lips ached for more, her body was on fire. She wanted him inside her.

"Someone will see us sneak away," she whispered.

"And they will be jealous." Gently, he tugged on her hand and urged her toward the stairs leading down into the garden. "For I steal away the prettiest girl at the ball."

Her feet felt as if they were floating as he led her from the veranda. If someone saw, she didn't know, or really cared. It was more her own determination that they have a slow courtship that she was utterly failing at, but desire flowed through every part of her.

He took her to the greenhouse, which was utterly dark. The door gave and he stepped inside, him just a shape in the darkness as he turned back to her, his arm holding the door open. "There won't be chaste kisses inside this door," he said as if warning her. His voice caressed down her spine, settling deep in her belly, where she wanted him most.

If she stepped inside, the distance between them would be gone. She would be accepting him in entirety, as he husband, her companion and her friend. And that distance they'd had between them couldn't be brought back—but did she want it to be? Was this desire not heavenly? Was being the one that basked in his attention not the best thing in the world? He would be hers and she would be his.

Tentatively, she took a step inside and he closed the door. It was quiet inside, as if they'd shut themselves away. Only a drop of water somewhere was heard, as if there was heavy anticipation in the air. Her body had grown heavy, her pulse beating steadily, through every part of her.

It was too dark for them to be seen. They were in essence alone, but there was no pretense of distance now. This was a man and a woman who loved each other and they were going to enact that union. In a grossly inappropriate manner and place, many would say. Right now, she didn't care about place or comfort. All she needed was seclusion.

"Caius," she said breathily. It broke the distance between them and he came to her. His lips and hands seeking her, her seeking him. The taste of him suffused her mind again, sweeping away everything that had been. It was him and her now, and nothing else mattered.

His hand at her neck, deepened the kiss as he drew her to him, her body molding to his, every taut plane and muscle of him. He led her somewhere, back until she felt something behind her, a potting table. Slipping up, she drew her knees up around him, feeling more of him to her, his hardness to her most sensitive part.

Sensations spiraled up her body, culminating with the draw from his lips, his hands. His warm hand roamed over the soft material of her dress, over the mound of her breast. How she wished it wasn't there, but it would be too cumbersome to take it off, and they were in too much of a hurry, because as his hips ground to hers, the heat inside her had roared into a fire.

At the same time, she had to feel him to her, and her sense faltered utterly as his lips stroked down the side of her neck, while his hips undulated to hers. "Please," she whispered, drawing her skirt up so her thighs were utterly revealed. Her damned undergarments were in the way, but he tugged them down and beneath her backside.

His breath was harsh and labored as he worked, returning to her as she was bare for him. Quickly unbuttoning his breeches, and then his tip was at her entrance, pushing in. It hurt because it had been so long, but she wouldn't trade it for anything in the world. It was impossibly sweet, the sensation so heady, she didn't know what to do with it. It radiated out through every part of her body and she groaned with the pleasure.

Her tender insides took every inch of him, stretching her to a fullness her body recalled. Her breath faltered as she held him to her. The pleasure was so very pointed, so sharp, she feared it would hurt, but the pain never came, only tension building higher. Pleasure reverberating through her every time he drew out and pushed in. It was like a storm that ebbed and surged, building higher and faster, gathering in intensity.

Her release started, waves of exquisite pleasure, moans escaping her with each one as he ground harder to her, until his body tensed. A moment of stillness until he quickened and released deep inside her, surges that brought renewed waves of pleasure for her.

Slowly they eased and shaky breath returned. His body shook with the last vestiges of his release. Senses were starting to reform and she sighed deeply with a deep sense of satisfaction. It felt almost a little like she'd been holding her breath all this time, to finally breathe easily.

Her arms refused to let him go and they stayed as they were for a moment as reality returned and she fully accepted that she'd just made love to Caius in someone's greenhouse, during a ball. Certainly not how she'd intended the evening to go, but she couldn't stop herself smiling.

Yes, her decision to keep him at arm's length, to slowly find themselves to each other had completely gone out the window. Perhaps it had been unrealistic.

Even so, she didn't regret what they'd just done. It felt so very right. They were together, in the way they could be, or perhaps couldn't help but to be.

"Is my hair horrid?" she asked.

"It is…" he said. "It's been worse."

There was reassurance if she'd ever heard it, she thought wryly. Luckily there was usually a maid available for such emergencies, like those produced by impromptu trysts in some dark corners. She really was a shocking guest—and not much to brag about as a chaperone as poor Jane had been entirely deserted. Hopefully Octavia was keeping an eye on her. Alright, maybe she was a little ashamed at the lack of fortitude she'd just shown. Had folded like wet paper—but she didn't regret it.

Chapter 38:

"WHERE HAVE YOU BEEN?" Octavia demanded when Caius returned to the ballroom. "You look flustered. Where's Eliza?"

"I believe she's sought the powder room," Caius said and surveyed the dancers. With Eliza out of the room, he lost interest completely.

"Is that so?" Octavia said. "Is she by chance looking a bit flustered too?"

"I couldn't possibly say," Caius said without inflection.

"I'm sure you couldn't."

Julius approached. "That girl is dancing with every man in the room."

"I told you she would charm them."

"Well, with any luck, we'll have her married off before the night is over so we can have our house back."

"Don't be ungenerous, Julius," Octavia chided. "Ah, there's Eliza. My, she is rosy-cheeked tonight."

The youngest part of him wanted to tell her to shut up, but he was no longer the young man who squabbled with his siblings. Mostly.

"How is Jane?" Eliza asked when she arrived.

"Dancing up a storm."

"Oh, good. I hope she's having a splendid time."

"Who is she, anyway?" Julius asked. "We know nothing about her, other than she is an orphan."

"She is our new illustrator. Incredibly gifted."

"Oh, that's lovely," Octavia said. "I adore people with talents. Don't you, Julius?"

Julius harrumphed. "How does one get some refreshments at this damned thing?"

"More importantly, have you managed to scribble your name on anyone's dance card yet?" Octavia asked.

"Eliza, would you care to dance at some point?" Julius asked.

"I'd be delighted."

"See," Julius said pointedly to Eliza. "Until then, if you need me, I will be in the cards room."

"We really cannot take him out of the house, can we?" Octavia complained.

A man approached and nervously asked Octavia if he could claim one of her dances and she kept him waiting for a moment while she made up her mind. "Well, I actually think I will ignore Matthew for this coming dance if you are quick."

The young man took that encouragement and led her onto the dance floor.

"Octavia is toying with the young men, I see," Eliza said.

"The worse she treats them, the more they seek her attention. Maybe that is true for all of us, but please don't take it to heart."

All he wanted was to put his arm around her and draw her close, but it was inappropriate. He supposed they would have to stay to the end of the ball, or however long Jane had dancing partners.

"Come back with us," he said after a moment of silence between them.

"Your carriage will not fit five people."

"Although if we leave early, it will have time to return for a second journey."

"Don't think our courtship is over simply because you had your way with me," she said pointedly.

"Maybe we could limit that courtship to say the hours before midnight?" he suggested.

"Oh, you think that would be a good solution?"

"I think that would be an excellent solution, else I will pine for you so deeply the angels will sigh for me."

"You do have a way with words. It's surprising you haven't excelled more in the field of love letters. One must wonder." She was teasing him now.

"I prefer my worship of your finest qualities to be more... physical."

The arrival of Jane paused their banter. "It's incredibly hot," she said, her cheeks rosy and a slight sheen on her upper lip.

"There is a veranda outside, but I wouldn't recommend it. It is known for stealing kisses."

"Really?" Jane said without an ounce of understanding that it was jest.

"Take Julius. You will be eminently safe with him," Caius recommended. "And he can glare at anyone who dares try to approach you."

"I don't think he likes me."

"Then you are in with every other person in the world."

Octavia joined them as well. "That man stood on my foot. I swear they should be certified as being able to dance before they let them in, as we are at risk of life and limb here. Where has that man with the champagne gone? Shall we go in search for him."

"It sounds like the best possible idea," Jane concurred.

"Then what shall we do for the rest of the evening?" Caius asked. "Another dance perhaps?"

"I don't know. I have promised the next dance to someone else," she said loftily.

"You wound me." He stepped closer and kissed her on her hair. "But not as much as if you leave me to pine for you tonight. Come home with me." Or he would be at risk of standing outside her window and mooning like a lunatic. His body simply refused to be without her now. He wanted her there to talk to, to sit with, to love and to laugh. "We should renew our vows."

"What?" she said, confused at how the topic had arisen. "You wish for us to wed again? That is awfully forward. One dance and you wish to wed?"

"Apparently one dance is all it takes." He leaned closer. "One dance and you might be carrying our child right now." The idea was more exciting than he could articulate. Him, her and a child. A family. It seemed almost too good to be true.

"I've made an utterly scandalous debutant," she lamented.

"Luckily I have the best of intentions."

"Then perhaps Paris in the spring?"

"Spring? We can leave tomorrow."

"No, what about Jane's debut? I promised her."

"Octavia can guard her."

"That is hardly suitable."

"True. Julius will simply have to chaperone both of them. I'm sure he'd be delighted."

The mirth at the idea made her eyes shine, because they both knew Julius would lament the cruelty of the world at having to chaperone his sister and houseguest singlehandedly.

"It will do him good," Caius concluded. "If you don't trust him, you can invite that woman you work with to stay with them."

"I think that wouldn't do at all. She has two children, and I expect she would have little tolerance for Julius."

"That may well be true. Or else, I could wait until spring, provided you come home with me tonight."

"So we are negotiating now?"

"No, that is utterly a pretense. At the end of the evening, I will heave you over my shoulder and carry you off. Fair warning."

"Brute."

"Now, don't be heartless and deny me this dance. And you shouldn't let Julius use you to ignore his social obligations."

Taking her by the hand, he led her onto the floor as the next dance was starting. By no means did he relish dancing, but doing so with Eliza made it utterly tolerable.

And it discouraged anyone from coming over to speak to them. Because he'd much rather talk about what they should do in Paris than to people wanting to know what to do with their investments. Maybe he could convince her to go in two weeks, or maybe a Christmas wedding. Could anything be more perfect?

Chapter 39:

SNOW FELL OUTSIDE THE large window in the small Patisserie she'd taken refuge in from the cold. Paris was utterly beautiful in winter. There were few tourists and the street were sparse.

Caius had told her he didn't wish her to join him in one particular store he was visiting, and now she was curious as she waited for him to join her.

"Un rafraîchissement pour madame?" a neatly dressed man asked, drawing her attention away from searching for Caius.

She ordered a hot chocolate, and her mind was drawn to the whiskey filled chocolates she'd seen. Caius would much prefer that to the sweet concoction she was about to be served, but in all honestly, he'd rather have the whiskey without the chocolate.

With a sigh, she turned her attention to the window and watched the streets outside. Cold emanated from the glass, but it was sufficiently warm in here. Her heart brightened when she saw him, a cold bluster making the snow whirl around him. He smiled when he saw her and her eyes followed him as he walked in through the door and took the seat opposite her.

"I didn't order anything for you. I thought after this we could find something with more stout refreshments."

"That would be immensely appreciated. But first, I want to give you this," he said, putting a small box on the table. The box was made with embroidered gold detail.

"Caius," she said, her insides clenching in excitement. He'd told her he was seeking a gift for her. In fact, he tended to find all sorts of curious gifts to give her. Pearl earrings back in London, an engraved silver box in Calais, and now this.

Opening the box, inside sat a small golden birdcage on top of a bed of black velvet. It was meticulous in detail and had a rounded top where a circle would take a chain at the very top. "It's beautiful."

"There's a little lever you can pull. There," he said, pointing to the impossibly small lever at the side. With her fingernail, she pulled it and the little golden bird flapped its wings. A small door opened the cage. "That is marvelous. Thank you. I will treasure it."

Her chocolate arrived and she carefully placed the small birdcage down on its bed. It was a gift that she could imagine a child would examine with wonder. Maybe their children. It hurt her heart to imagine it. She would have to show it to Rosie and Philip when she saw them next.

Caius was regarding her. "What?" she asked.

"Nothing," he said with a smile. "Do you wish to go to the theater tonight?"

"That could be nice."

It had been a long time since she'd had nothing particular to do. They could just roam the city and do whatever pleased them. Back in London, she'd tended to stay with Caius every night, but come morning, she'd returned to her house and business. They'd existed in a strange in-between state, being half together as a couple but not fully.

It hadn't been her intention, but come the evening and the dark, she ached for him, an ache so compelling it drove her into his arms every night.

"I am too impatient," Caius had declared one morning with finality, then he'd stolen her away across the channel where no distractions drew her away and they could spend long, lazy days together in a wintery city.

"Perhaps we should buy a gift for Octavia as well, because I expect she's less than pleased we've snuck away to Paris with barely any notice. She'll say we've eloped."

"One cannot elope with one's wife. In terms of planning a wedding, which is what she really wants, she is going to have to organise her own. I expect that would be a much easier task than facilitating Julius'," Caius said tartly. "Although I'll commend her if she achieves it."

They had been to quite a few balls, and while Jane had enjoyed every one of them, Julius had danced with barely a handful of people, and he'd lamented each one. "Yes," Eliza said with a sigh. Getting Julius to be an active participant in his search for a wife was proving difficult.

The hot chocolate was warming her and she sighed with contentment. "It is a beautiful city."

"We don't have to go home, you know," Caius said.

The idea was shocking to her for a moment. Her mind raced, thinking of all the things the business needed. Teresa would balk at the notion, but would she really? Teresa was there to manage things, and she was perfectly capable of doing what needed to be done. The business wouldn't fall to pieces without her.

Maybe it was that last step away from safety that gave her pause. If she handed the reins of the business to Teresa, which she could do without any great impact, then she would have to fully embrace being Lady Warwick. It was a reality she'd been aware of, but hadn't fully come to terms with. The truth was, though, that if she was to accept him and this marriage to the full extent, she would have to embrace the identity that came with it.

"We could go further south. Italy. Maybe find our way down to the Mediterranean."

The proposition was so tempting. They could just be the two of them for a while longer, learn to be a couple again without the distractions of Jane and Julius, Octavia and the business. It would be so easy to get caught up in what everyone else needed and should do. And Italy—she'd only ever dreamt she would see it. "They don't need us, do they?"

"I think at times it is better to let everyone tread water for themselves."

"Is that what we are doing? Treading water?"

"Yes, and we are doing so marvelously. Now, let's walk along the Seine and see what we find. We have a few hours before supper."

Finishing the last of her chocolate, she rose and her hand snuck into the crook of his elbow, where it felt so natural for her to be. Was there anything better than a leisurely walk in the snow? No, she couldn't think of it.

Epilogue

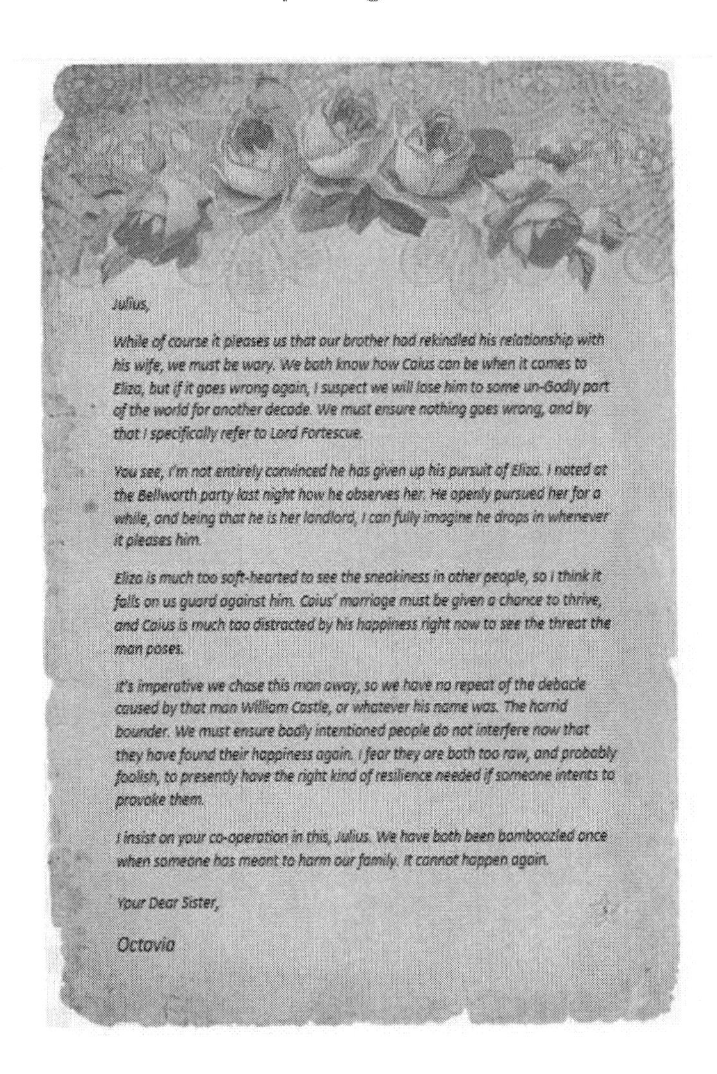

Julius,

While of course it pleases us that our brother had rekindled his relationship with his wife, we must be wary. We both know how Caius can be when it comes to Eliza, but if it goes wrong again, I suspect we will lose him to some un-Godly part of the world for another decade. We must ensure nothing goes wrong, and by that I specifically refer to Lord Fortescue.

You see, I'm not entirely convinced he has given up his pursuit of Eliza. I noted at the Bellworth party last night how he observes her. He openly pursued her for a while, and being that he is her landlord, I can fully imagine he drops in whenever it pleases him.

Eliza is much too soft-hearted to see the sneakiness in other people, so I think it falls on us guard against him. Caius' marriage must be given a chance to thrive, and Caius is much too distracted by his happiness right now to see the threat the man poses.

It's imperative we chase this man away, so we have no repeat of the debacle caused by that man William Castle, or whatever his name was. The horrid bounder. We must ensure badly intentioned people do not interfere now that they have found their happiness again. I fear they are both too raw, and probably foolish, to presently have the right kind of resilience needed if someone intents to provoke them.

I insist on your co-operation in this, Julius. We have both been bamboozled once when someone has meant to harm our family. It cannot happen again.

Your Dear Sister,

Octavia

Join my readers' group at www.camilleoster.com

Other Books by Camille Oster

An Absent Wife - The desertion of his wife came as a complete surprise to Lord Lysander Warburton, even as he readily admits he never excelled as a husband. Running off with a lowly lieutenant was in line with her consistent talent for being disagreeable. Never more so when he learns her supposed demise from cholera turns out not to be true. Unfortunately there is no choice but to retrieve his troublesome and wayward wife.

The Discarded Wife - Victorian London is a cruel place for a divorcee, but with the death of Sophie Duthie's beloved second husband, she is now a widow, and independent for the first time in her life. She might not have much in terms of means, but with the help of her music shop, she can support herself and her son, Alfie. Even though her second marriage was happy, Sophie is done with husbands. Her first marriage taught her well that fairy tales are nothing more than illusions.

To Lord Aberley, his former wife is nothing but a scheming pariah, and unfortunately, his subsequent engagement wasn't successful—not that he's ever had much delusions about marriage. It is something he now wishes to avoid at all costs, but he needs an heir. It is the one duty he cannot overlook, so learning that his former wife's son is six years old, creates serious doubt about his true parentage. Seeing the child only confirms it. Alfie Duthie is his child.

Amongst Silk and Spice - Sir Hugo Beauford had no idea what to expect when the king summoned him from Calais, away from the battles securing the French throne for their English king. A quest to find the Earl of Chanderling's wayward daughter was not something he wanted, but being a knight in the king's service, he was duty-bound to fulfill his king's wishes - even if the bothersome girl he remembered had last been heard of in Venice. He'd never had plans to travel as far east as Venice, let alone much farther as this quest took more effort than he could have imagined - including dragging an unwilling and continuously challenging young woman across the known world.

Manufactured by Amazon.ca
Bolton, ON

18546829R00142